SPUNGUNION

PRAISE FOR SPUNGUNION

"It moves, it's tender, it has a texture to it, a perspective, a smell, an atmosphere of fragile heartbreak and queasy unease. It's Joe R. Lansdale good. I adored it."—Aaron Dries, Author, *A Place For Sinners* and *House Of Sighs*

"A fever dream that's hauled on 18 wheels, *Spungunion* is pure, country-fried, existential horror! And Boden cracks its reigns with razor-sharp prose!"—Kristopher Triana, Author of *The Ruin Season* and *Growing Dark*

"A mixture of a modern *Odyssey*, a bleak *Wizard of Oz* and a more linear *Jacob's Ladder*. It's grim."—Christopher Ropes, Author of *The Operating Theater* and *Complicity*

"*Spungunion* is a surprisingly poignant heartfelt novella. Folksy and bittersweet, it's humming with beautiful prose and achingly haunting imagery. Boden has created an epic trucker mythology, one that sings with the twang of a folk tale or a plaintive country song lamenting the travails of lost love. This is a darkly fantastic trip filled with horror and loneliness, where revenge and scapegoats lure good folks into committing evil wrongs, where shadows and loss hitchhike from the outskirts of cracked macadam roads that lead to space-black regions."—Christopher Slatsky, author of *Alectryomancer And Other Weird Tales*

"John Boden is a writer to watch. *Spungunion* is stylish and lyrical, yet down and dirty. Boden sends readers on a journey through a bizarre landscape of terrifying sights and beings, creatures that may have once been human but are now wholly unnatural. In short, *Spungunion* is an outstanding dark, rural fantasy, and you need to read it."—Lee Thomas, Bram Stoker Award and Lambda Literary Award-winning author of *The German* and *Down on Your Knees*.

"*Spungunion* is a wonderful countrified tale of darkness, depravity and revenge. It packs all the flavor of a greasy chicken-fried steak into one hell of an entertaining package. It's Neil Gaiman by way of Red Simpson."—Amber Fallon, Author of *The Terminal* and *The Warblers.*

"*Spungunion* is a page-turner and a house burner—everything about this story demonstrated the arrival of a new talent. The narrative voice, the pacing, the original take on mythology... it all adds up to a whole greater than the sum of its parts. It's a fable wrapped in folklore inside a fantasy. Clever and poignant and at times funny, this thing twists and turns like the river Lethe, pulling the reader into the darkness of Deke larch's own private Hades. Simply Brilliant."—Matthew Darst, Author of *Freaks Anon* and *Dead Things*

"Southern gothic meets Bradbury down a very dark road long last twilight, and the shadows are alive. Dark, lyrical and tender yet savage, this blue collar tale of loss, love and the quest for answers is affecting, haunting and scary as hell. I loved it."—Kit Power, Author of *Breaking Point*.

"This trucker's tale of bloody revenge and harrowing self-illumination takes place in the deepest, strangest veins of the Twilight Zone's midnight highways. Boden rolls his supernatural mystery down the blacktop surface of the road to Hell, and you're gonna love the journey into the fire."—Philip Fracassi, author of *Behold the Void, Fragile Dreams* and *Altar.*

"John Boden writes like he's a dealer at a big money poker game. Every page, like every card, ups the stakes, and the reader can't wait to see what happens next. *Spungunion* is a welcome addition to the road trip/trucker sub-genre. It's creepy as hell and the ride is well worth the price of admission."—Sam W. Anderson, Author of *The Nines* and *American Gommorah*.

FUNGASM PRESS
an imprint of Eraserhead Press
PO Box 10065
Portland, OR 97296

www.fungasmpress.com
facebook/fungasmpress

ISBN: 978-1-62105-298-2
Copyright © 2019 by John Boden
Cover art copyright © 2019 Matthew Revert
Edited by John Skipp

All rights reserved. No part of this book may be reproduced or transmitted in any form or by any means, electronic or mechanical, including photocopying, recording, or by any information storage and retrieval system, without the written consent of the publisher, except where permitted by law.

Printed in the USA.

SPUNGUNION

JOHN BODEN

DARK LIKE MURDER BALLADS

an introduction
by Bracken MacLeod

There are questions every writer hears with some frequency. And while "Where do you get your ideas?" has fallen out of vogue, there are still several that get asked so often, you can almost count them down. Lately, the one I hear the most is, "Do you listen to music when you write?" If you say yes, it's inevitably followed up with, "What kind?" While the answers are an interesting bit of trivia—even if they don't have much to say about a writer's quality—I think there is something about the line of inquiry that's very telling. That is, it brings to light the inkling people have that music and prose are complimentary art forms—that one can inform and enrich the other.

I like this idea, because it suggests that deep down, people get that, line by line, writers are often working with sentence structure, cadence, and word choice in a way that reflects how rhythm and melody work in a song. And what we call literary "voice" can be analogized to the idea of a particular band's overall style. Some writers—the really good ones—have such a signature sound you can tell who they are by reading a paragraph by itself. Think of Cormac McCarthy or Stephen King. Both have unique voices that come through in the work. Those two are innovators, too. Lots of people try to play like King because he's inspired so many, but you can still tell when you're reading him. His work always sounds like the original. I'm reminded in that instance of Charles Mingus' line about Charlie Parker: "If Charlie Parker was a gunslinger there'd be a whole lot of dead copycats."

My point is this: when I listen to Tom Waits, Wynton Marsalis, or Wolves in the Throne Room, the music connects in a way that wakes some part of me. It stirs a feeling deep down. And in the same way I listen to certain musical artists because their style reflects or affects the mood I'm in, I read specific writers because I can rely on their words to always make me feel a particular way or see things from a fresh viewpoint—they scratch that part of my consciousness that itches.

John Boden's work is like that.

He writes melancholy like nobody I know. His sound is often that kind of mournful wail like Chet Baker played on "Alone Together." It's sincere and isn't laden with a bunch of shallow sentimentality undermining its impact. That song is like mainlining grief. And when Boden wants to, he perfectly captures that exact same sensibility. He strips sadness bare and lays it out in a way that's stark and impacting. When that cat plays, you're really going to feel it. Don't misunderstand me, though. Boden's no one note performer. The guy has chops across styles.

The first thing I ever read of his was the story, "Intruder," in John Skipp's gargantuan anthology, Psychos. It's a mixture of home invasion terror and quirky character study of a hapless sufferer of Obsessive Compulsive Disorder. And though the story is, at its heart, deeply threatening, there's a playfulness that skirts around the edges. The balance between those two moods is perfectly set. Boden knows exactly when to go for the laugh and when land a gut punch. It's like a song where the hook is good, but damn man, that chorus! Being a musician himself, I know exactly why Skipp has an ear for Boden's style.

He loves to play with other artists who make him think, feel, and want to sit in for that set. Not only did he select John's story for Psychos, he edited this book too. He clearly knows when he's listening to a player who can really hang.

By contrast, Dominoes is a 180-degree shift in direction from the narratively direct "Intruder." Dominoes is a dark interpretation of a Little Golden Book ("A Little Horror Book" as labelled by the publisher, Shock Totem). But what sets it apart from other satirical "children's" works like Pat the Zombie, Go the Fuck to Sleep, or If You Give Mommy a Glass of Wine is that this book is a legitimate collection of carefully crafted prose poetry. While the external presentation is parodical, the work inside is profoundly disturbing and beautiful like the delicate corpse of a dead bird in the road. Boden goes to places in this book that are nightmarish, haunting, and absurd. Did I mention that it's dark? Angry death metal dark.

His novella, Jedi Summer with the Magnetic Kid is less death metal and more like a classic rock song about the brevity of youth and its promises. Jedi Summer (and how I wish he'd named it "Summerland" after the King's X song, like he'd once told me he might) straddles the line also between memoir and fiction, giving us a hint of John's own childhood in the summer of 1983, but one that seems just a little off. He offers honest self-reflection seasoned with an uncanniness that weaves throughout in a discordant leitmotif that keeps the reader wondering exactly where fact and fiction meet.

As you might predict by this point, the book you hold in your hands, Spungunion, is another change in style and direction, but one that keeps that signature sound, the tone that's recognizably John Boden's. It's at once wry, dark, and melancholy. This work is structurally more in line with "Intruder" or our collaboration for Shock Totem's special holiday issue, "Halloween On…" (and working with him was all treat, without a hint of trick) than either Dominoes or Jedi Summer. But don't let that mislead you. Even if it is a return to a more traditional narrative style, this isn't like what you've read before.

And as an added treat, this book includes a bonus short story I first read years ago, that I've long championed as one of my favorites of his. A lost B-Side. It's a wonderful, short riff with a kind of sensibility reminiscent of Stephen King's early style. Boden's no imitator, though. "The Drawer" is him taking a beloved standard and putting his own mark on it—a fresh take on a classic piece—and he nails it like only someone who really loves that song can.

I'm not going to spoil this book by going into any more detail about either this book or its bonus track. You want to go into this fresh. But what I am going to do is make a suggestion.

Read this book in a room with a record player.

Warm vinyl and good speakers are what every copy of Spungunion ought to come with. This book wants to be read with Nick Cave and the Bad Seeds backing it up. The pages that follow have a tone like Johnny Cash's American recordings and Danzig's eponymous album. They're stripped down and honky tonk dark like murder ballads sung by a guy who smokes too much. No pretense; all heart and passion.

John's getting ready to play a whole new set of material. But before you turn to the next page, you should order your drink now, because once he starts to play, you're not going to want to miss a note.

Bracken MacLeod
Sudbury, Massachusetts
7 September 2018

DEDICATION

This work is dedicated to my father, for who I am named and hopefully doing proud. The road we walked together through life was a lot shorter than I had ever hoped it'd be. It was not a smooth one but it was one I would never trade for something better paved. I love you , Dad and miss you always. I owe you so very much. I cannot wait to see you again one day.

And also to my Pap, Ralph Rutter. He was a trucker and a giant of a man. Gruff and no nonsense but loving when it mattered. I used to listen to his trucker tapes and that's where my love of that music came from. This is for him as well.

And also, also—again—for my pal, Jim Boyer. I miss him a lot. One of the truest friends I ever had. I put you into this thing and I think you come off pretty good.

SPUNGUNION

(*pronounced:* Spun-Gun-Yun*) noun;*

1. A dish made from rotting road kill, usually a skunk or a opossum. The more fragrant or maggoty, the better.

2. Something that's been on the road for a long and unfortunate time.

I. The Winding Up

*"Now boys don't start to ramblin' round,
On this road of sin are you sorrow bound..."*
-Leon Payne

ONE

Deke Larch stayed down near the end of the last row in Morning Glory Trailer Park. He wasn't there most mornings, so whether or not they were glorious he couldn't say. He doubted it. He could confirm that no glory visited his trailer. Not in the last two years anyway. His was the least modern of the block. The trailer wasn't an absolute shithole, but it was pretty close. Hell, if you added up all the time he got to spend there over a month, you might come up with a whole day or two, maybe three if there was a lot of rain. He was a road dog, what the oldsters used to call a gear jammer. Truck Driver Numero Uno. He didn't entertain and he wasn't holding a shoot for *Better Homes & Gardens* so fuck it. It was a place for him to sleep when he could, eat when he needed to and to put his pot to piss in. It hadn't been his castle for quite a while, not since someone killed his queen.

Deke sat on the four plastic-wrapped cases of *Chunky* soup, all of them vegetable beef, and smoked his cigarette. The Viceroy hung from the corner of his downturned mouth as he stacked the bills on the card table before him. "Fuckers," he grumbled as he added up the utilities for a place he barely even lived in. His nostrils flared as the acrid smoke grew darker, letting him know that his smoke had burned down to the filter. He pinched it between calloused fingers and dropped it onto the paper plate with the remains of his lunch. Stale bread crusts mourned the dying butt. Deke went back to his accounting. A breeze trickled through the torn screen door, from the sewage plant side by the smell of it. Last year's dirty plastic crinkled and sighed in the slight wind. Out of the filthy window above the table, through the run on sentences of fly shit speckles and the hornet husk punctuation, he saw the black car at the end of the drive way. He was familiar with the vehicle after seeing it nearly a hundred times here and on the road, parked along certain off ramps, in the parking lot of Darst Diner, a few times on the street by the Hub. One year and eight months and the assholes were still watching him. They knew he hadn't done anything, He assumed they were just waiting for that last pin to work its way out of the cog, for him to finally lose his shit. He cursed under his breath and went back to the bills. Tore open the envelope from *Light Brothers Heating & Furnace Company,* their cartoon faces on the front. He read the amount they claimed he owed and snorted through clenched teeth. "So much for dead dinosaurs."

He dropped the invoice from the oil company back on the table and surveyed his surroundings. A falling apart sofa that slumped in the corner of the room like a dead rhinoceros, a few folding chairs. His card tables, two pushed together to almost make an honest-to-God real sized table. A stack of canned soup next to two stacks of beer and two jugs of water. A small TV sitting on top of a floor model television that had been non-functional for about four years. Pictures of sunsets on the smoke-tarnished walls. Dark crème colored drapes that were actually nicotine-stained white. His kingdom. This King was far from proud. He scraped a chunk of dried mud from the bottom of his boot, dragging the worn sole along the corner of the case of Schlitz beside him. The whiff that touched his nose let him know it wasn't mud. "Damn dogs," he grumbled. He went back to the bills.

From back of the hall came a loud ringing—his alarm clock. One of the old-time wind-up with bells on top variety. Deke could never drag himself awake to the timid beep of a digital alarm clock. It was letting him know it was time for him to get up and get ready to head back out on the road. Would be, had he ever gone to bed.

Deke sighed and stomped back down the hall. He kicked the clock from its perch on the milk crate that served as his nightstand and watched it smash against the paneled wall. "Time flies," he chuckled. But the chuckle died when he looked at the mattress with its great smears of dark brown staining the top and side. All that he had to remember his sweet Lucille by, aside from the picture of her on the pillow, and that was worn to white paper where he rubbed it with a calloused thumb every night. He went out and bought a frame to keep from ruining the picture completely. The cops had thought him crazy when he told them he had no plans to get rid of it.

"You need to burn that thing and buy a new one," Deputy Fallon had urged.

"That's got to be some kind of hazard," the other younger cop, Williamson, had argued. Deke had just stared the men down until they got in their cruisers and pissed off. After they'd taken all their pictures and done all their forensical hoodoo, he put it right back on the springs and cried himself to sleep, tossing and turning next to the side where she had slept—hand on the very spot where her life drained away. He did it every night he wasn't on the road.

The clock finished its cacophonous demise and Deke stood in the silence it left behind. He felt the tears begin along with the tiredly familiar tightness in his barrel chest. He pushed his closed eyes with smoke-yellowed fingers and sat down hard on the edge of the bed. The stained mattress molding to his ass, he tossed aside filthy sheets and lay back against the flattened pillow. Beside him on the bed was the picture of Lucille, his dead wife. He touched the glass that protected it with the back of his hand. With his other hand, he grazed the fading stain with slow fingers. He smiled thinly and closed his eyes and within minutes, he was asleep and in his dreams, Lucille was with him.

TWO

It was dark when he woke up but he was no longer able to gauge the passing of time. Time was just something that shambled and dragged on behind him like so much mummy bandage. The phone was ringing, again or still, as Deke dragged his bulk out of bed and lumbered towards the living room. "Yes," he growled, nearly yanking the thing from the wall.

"Where the fuck are you?!" the phlegmy voice on the other end demanded. It was Boyer.

"I fell asleep, I'll grab a shower and be right there." Deke pushed greasy hair back over his forehead. He found he couldn't remember when he'd washed it last.

"Fuck the shower, Deke. You get clean on your own time. You been supposed to be on mine for the last three fucking hours!" A raspy sigh as the old man took a deep drag from his ever-present cigarillo. Deke closed his eyes and could almost smell its reek.

"Tiny's getting ready to go. He has three trailers to haul tonight and can't cover again if you don't get here."

Deke counted to five in his head and exhaled slowly through his nose. "I'll be right there, boss. Sorry." He looked at the stove, the radio on the counter, anywhere to keep his temper from getting out.

On the other end of the phone, the man sucked in more smoke. Blew it out. It sounded like a ghostly breeze in Deke's head. "You know what, Deeky. You had a shit year, almost *two*. I'm sorry for being a hard ass. You know I don't mean it. I'm just a gruff sonofabitch. S'why no one likes me. Take the shower but make it a quickie. Then be here at the hub by ten. Cool?" The man chuckled which mutated into a thick coughing fit.

Deke closed stinging eyes and felt a bit of sleep crust fall from the corner of his left.

"Ok. See you in a bit. Thanks."

He put the phone down without giving Boyer the final word. The hallway seemed to elongate as he trudged back to the bathroom. It was that way with nearly everything these days.

THREE

The night Lucille was killed, Deke pulled up to the dock and handed Smitty the sheaf of documents and papers from the Clifton Heights run. He was helping the old man put down the dock plate when the window above opened and Boyer poked his head out. Deke cringed as this usually meant a verbal assault with a side of profanity was coming his way. Boyer just looked at him, face pastier than usual, flesh competing with the shock of white hair that haloed it.

"Deke," he spoke, softly.

Deke looked around and noticed that the others had all stopped and were watching, those who weren't staring at their boots. Yardley, Lutzke and Janz were like department store mannequins. Fazz was at the snack machine, frozen in the act of feeding a quarter into it. Vajda was nowhere in sight which only meant he was in the shitter. Jones sat on the sofa pretending to read the issue of Reader's Digest that had done time on the crate-that-was-used-as-a-table for the last six years.

Deke made a mental note that not a soul had uttered a word to him since his entrance. Which was more than a little weird. His stomach began to twist and turn like a worm suddenly exposed when someone lifts the rock it lives beneath.

"Come up." Boyer finished and pulled the window closed. The sound of Deke's heavy feet on the wooden steps echoed through the hub. Seconds later, the sound they made would amount to nothing when he began to wail. All around the hub, nobody moved.

They always say that there is a sense to be had when something terrible happens to someone you love, countless film scenes and written works go on about "having a feeling something was amiss..." The reality is this: Life is just a balloon floating dangerously in a roomful of lit cigarettes. At any moment, second, day or week, *Pop!* And then everything as you know it is different or gone. Sometimes both.

Boyer had driven him home. This was a favor of untold greatness as Boyer did his best to not interact with anyone outside of work. Ever. He was a nice guy and a decent human being but a bit of an introvert. He was smarter than you could fathom and meaner than you want to. If he liked you, and he did Deke, you had no worries about who would hold you up in a struggle.

"I'll wait here," Boyer said and lit one of his little cigars.

Deke looked at him with sand blasted eyes and got out. The sound of the door slam was a shot in the dark. He stood for a second and felt his guts melt. He turned and leaned into the open car window.

"Go back," he said to Boyer and to himself and pinched the meat of his thigh with strong fingers. He stood up again and started walking, inside feeling like that balloon in that room full of cigarettes. Boyer stayed and watched him through the windshield.

There were three cruisers parked in front of the trailer. Two deputies stood on his porch. The older man, the one he presumed to be the sheriff stood, holding his hat, sadly clichéd, and stepped towards Deke with a hand outstretched.

"I'm Sheriff MacLeod," he offered and Deke saw the man's eyes were rimmed with wet. "I'm so sorry, Mr. Larch," His voice was the sound of pages turning in the dark. Deke looked at him and tried to speak, but there was nothing, so he just started up the steps.

"The neighbors, over there," the young deputy who stood off to the side, started while pointing over to the Wehunts, where they stood on their porch. Maggie had her head on Lloyd's shoulder. They could have been Siamese twins.

"In a minute," Deke said and pushed open the outer door.

He never even registered the six inch cut in the screen. He looked around at the men standing in his home. They all looked frightened and damned if they shouldn't. This was his home, and whatever happened they shouldn't be here—couldn't be here. He was going to walk back that hallway and go into the bedroom and Lucille would be sleeping, with the little television on, volume turned to nil. She'd be wearing one of his flannel shirts because she said she missed the smell of him when he was away. The flicker from *All in the Family* reruns strobing her slumber. He was thinking like a highway being eaten in miles. He pushed back the curtain and the floor fell out of his world, and out of the world he fell into and then the one beneath that. Deke had never really known what falling was until that moment. *Pop!*

FOUR

The pole light hum through the open window of the truck was the only sound in the cab. The Viceroy between his fingers was setting free a ghost of smoke. It snaked its way up and into the night. Deke smoked and stared at the building. J. B. Trucking and Movement Company: The Hub, as they called it. He took a final drag and flicked the butt onto the macadam. He opened the door and hopped down, his boots thunking and his knees bending slightly with audible pops. He stepped on the smoldering cigarette and walked in to see his boss. Above his head, bats dined and stars blinked out.

"Finally," said the portly man behind the desk. Deke tried to smile but it felt like a sweater that had shrunk, tight and uncomfortable and threatening to split and tear and making you look oh-so- foolish.

"Boyer," he managed.

"I know you've had a shitty run of it. Fuck, I liked Lucille. But sitting around and wallowing isn't helping you any. Sure as shit isn't helping me get stuff out and to where it's supposed to go." He sipped the glass on his desk, schnapps, more than likely. His eyes narrowed a bit and a thin sad, smile slithered over his lips. "Look, I need you… and I think I can help you stick a fork in this thing. You see Tiny down there when you came in?"

"No, probably in the can, he's a shitty bastard." Deke didn't even crack a smile when he said it. "All the chili dogs and beer, I'd wager."

Boyer smiled and nodded. "Before you get your papers and docs from Smitty, go talk with Tiny. You know his route, what he does. I'm thinking he may be able to tell you something. Help you, maybe."

There was a lot of unspoken laced throughout their short and awkward conversation. These sorts of discussions happened in the Hub from time to time, no one wanted to put a face on the doll and speak of things aloud, but they all knew of it.

They knew Tiny Smalls rode the Soul Road—the name they had given his route, his for as long as they could remember. They knew what he transported, why his runs were in the dead of night and why his clipboard always had a sulfurous reek. Numbers and dates scrawled on his paperwork in thick black ink that smelled like coal. Sometimes in dead languages. Tiny rode the Soul Road. That was his lot.

"Tiny," Deke managed when the giant stepped out from behind the metal door and closed his locker. The nine crucifixes that hung on the inside of it clanged like chimes.

He stood and stared at Deke for a minute that felt like hours. "Hey," he said. There was a sadness in his face, part of his empathetic way.

Tiny stood close to seven feet tall and weighed in at about four hundred and six pounds. A big man with a bigger heart and a job he wouldn't wish on his worst enemy but one that was destined just for him.

"I'm sorry," he said and clapped a hand the size of a catcher's mitt onto Deke's shoulder. Deke almost went down under the weight of it. "I've meant to wait for you, tell you I was sorry. I liked Lucille. You know how it is. You wanna let a person know you care, that you're thinkin' about them but everything you come up with in your head sounds so trite and stupid. So you say nothing. Nothing. And time just keeps swallowin' its tail." Tiny looked down at his feet.

"Thanks," Deke said as he mentally willed his knees not to buckle.

The two men had moved out onto the dock. The night was cool and the brightness of the lights bathed them in a yellow blanket. Tiny stood, hands in the pockets of his overalls, while Deke smoked. Tiny's forehead was wrinkled and creased like a bellows, his eyes so heavy and full of sadness they almost oozed it. Deke flicked the butt out into the back lot and sniffed. The air was chilled and felt good on his sinuses.

"So can you?" he asked again. He kicked at a bottle cap that lay near the toe of his boot; it skittered like a tiny crab and dove from the dock into shadow. Tiny said nothing; his lower lip trembled, almost like a tic.

The breeze stopped, and in the pocket of silence that dropped, Deke could hear a faint whisper coming from the giant before him. Prayers—the man was praying. He held up a finger, a crooked twig of a digit, and Deke knew he meant for him to be patient and wait. So, he did. Bats flitted in and out of the halo of light, eating gnats and bugs and possibly prayers.

"How long is your run tonight?" Tiny's voice was an icy hand on his neck, he'd been quiet for so long.

Deke shook his head a little, snapping back to the moment at hand. "Just down outside of Baltimore and back. I'm tired so I might stop and sleep after I deliver. I'll be home by mid-day tomorrow." He smiled a pleading smile and hoped the large man picked up on it. "I'll meet you here tomorrow night, about eleven." He looked towards the door and back.

"Bring me something of Lucille's. Something that was close. And don't ask me nothing." He held out his hand which swallowed Deke's own like a big fish eating a smaller one. Deke opened his mouth intending to thank the giant-of-a-man but nothing came out. Tiny gazed down at his friend, his cheeks slick with tears and a smile that showed his teeth. "That'll do." They went back inside.

Deke drove to Haddon, Maryland in a fog. He remembered nearly nothing of the drive, the delivery to Newman & Sons furniture or the return run. That was something he always found unsettling; pulling in somewhere and realizing that you had zoned out behind the wheel. Did you stop for red lights? Stop signs? How the hell did you know where you were going? But tonight, he was too preoccupied to be unnerved by his pre-occupation. The Mack turned back onto the road towards the trailer park. Deke yawned and knew that sleep would entangle him quickly. He pulled the truck into the yard and cut the engine. Like a strangled beast the engine's grumble died quickly. He walked around and up the steps to the door. He looked over and saw Lloyd peering out their kitchen window. He held his hand up in greeting and Deke did the same. He looked at the morning sun, hanging low and brightening. He went inside and was asleep as soon as he sat down, only succeeding in the removal of one boot.

FIVE

Tiny stood beside the cab of his Peterbilt. The rig could have been a dinosaur; it was ancient and looked every day of it. The once-red paint was cracked and peeling like dead skin. The only portion that was untouched was the drivers' side door, which was a sunburst of orange, gold and red with thick black script that read: *A Tombstone Every Mile.*

Deke smiled. He loved all the old songs, they were all he played in his truck: Del Reeves, Red Sovine, Billy Joe Shaver, Loretta Lynn and Waylon and Willie. He reached into his flannel shirt pocket and removed the ball. He'd woken up around sunset and made it for Tiny. It was the closest thing he could come up with. The cloth was from her old diner uniform. It had hung in the closet behind his suit for years.

It takes a special kind of woman to marry a truck driver, an even more special kind to stay with him. Lucille was that shade and several more. She was amazing. Deke met her when he was a freshman, not in school, but when his CDL was still new and clipped to his visor for the world to bow down to. His Mack was a shining sharp beast that cut down the highways and bi-ways of the east coast, hauling whatever needed to get from point A to point B. That greasy, grimy thing that lived on top of his head, the thing that was once a hat, had actually been newish and clean then. He'd weighed twenty pounds less and still smiled once in a while.

He had wanted to hit the Hidd'n Valley Restaurant but got held up in roadwork traffic and they were closed when he rolled up, so he stopped at Kuppy's for a late meal. And when the plate of country fried steak and potatoes was set before him, his eyes followed the slender hand that delivered it up to the shoulder that met the neck that held the head which had the sweetest smile he'd ever seen. Beneath the palest grey eyes. She killed him in that moment, stabbed his heart with a spike of love-at-first-sight that one only sees in shitty movies. His heart hurt so bad, he almost looked to make sure he wasn't bleeding into his food.

"Thanks, Ma'am" he stammered and felt like a slug under a terrifying salt shaker. He wanted to look away more than anything, but he couldn't. My God, she was beautiful.

"Is my Mom here?" She giggled. "What's with the Ma'am jazz?" She clapped his beefy shoulder with that angelic hand and giggled again. Sweat broke out and dampened Deke's back. He drew in a quick breath. "My name's Lucille. And I don't bite so don't look so scared." She patted him again and withdrew her touch.

Deke blinked about six times and choked out his reply: "I'm Deke. Hi."

He went to work cutting through the breading on his steak and kicked himself to death inside for not being able to look her in the eyes. He took a furtive bite and chewed it slowly, making sure to keep his mouth closed. She watched for a second before picking up her pen and rag and moving down to wipe the counter.

She tipped her head back at him and smiled, "Aw… a shy boy." She chuckled and went back through to the kitchen. Deke finished his plate and wished he wasn't an idiot.

The guts of the ball were made up of hair from her brush, a few bristles from her toothbrush, a button from the blood-stained mattress and a page from her favorite book, *The Stories Of H.H Munro*. He had wrapped them in the mint green cloth and sewed it up with loping uneven stitches. It felt warm in his hand yet his breath shown in the darkness as white wisps. Autumn was definitely swinging in, hard.

Tiny held out a hand, like a great upturned bowl of calloused skin and nodded for Deke to put the ball inside. Deke dropped it and the big hand swallowed it up like time. Tiny closed his eyes and nodded his head slightly. Deke watched him and felt the air thicken around them. The quiet grew louder, a blind hiss that you felt in your teeth and bones but that made no sound at all.

When Tiny opened his eyes, everything returned at once. The few crickets and sounds from the highway rushed back in a torrent. "This will work." Tiny sighed and it sounded like he held all of the anguish in the world. "When you come in tomorrow for your papers to run, there'll be an envelope with 'em. Don't open it here. Leave here and stop at the first church you see. Some place somewhat sacred. Sit upon the steps and read the contents. Then you will begin a journey, almost like a quest."

Deke cocked an eyebrow and smiled, almost. "What?"

"Look. This ain't funny. You know I shouldn't be doing any of this. Boyer should never have sent you to me. He knows better, So do you. You know what I do." Tiny lowered his voice and continued, "I deliver the damned. That's what the Soul Road is. You know that, and I have certain, um, acquaintances that may be able to help you, but they ain't gonna just spell it out for ya. Some of them is nasty business and like to play games. But most won't. Think of 'em as candles put here to help light the way for you. I asked special permission to put you in contact with them." He stopped and swallowed, it clicked loudly. "Just follow the rules. Anything I say to do or they tell you to do, do it. Just how they say to. There's a reason or it wouldn't be that way." He lowered his enormous head and beneath the thin strands of silver hair Deke noticed the lace of scars that covered his scalp.

"Thanks, okay. I get it," was all he said.

Deke chewed on his dry lip and looked at the giant. "What's it like, Tiny?" He jacked a thumb towards the rig parked along the chain link, the moans and groans that leaked from it like toxic fumes. Tiny kicked the toe of a boot against the cement. The boot was so worn that the steel in the toe was visible. He narrowed eyes and almost smiled at Deke.

"Ain't nobody gonna squall louder than someone who's had their whole lives to make it right and pissed it all away at every turn. Regret is a splinter that goes hard and deep, brother. And if you ain't careful, it'll nail you to the wall." Tiny stuck his hands in his pockets and turned to the truck. "I still try and I know it ain't true but I sometimes think I run outta pity years ago."

Deke's face darkened like a sky promising a storm, "You ever get any cargo you know?" The words stung rolling from his tongue, and from the look on Tiny's face, the sting wasn't lost in travel.

"Every so often. Can't be helped. But all I can do is count 'em and seal the door. Gotta be just another load." He scratched his chin; the white whiskers that lived there hardly moved. They stood in a bubble of encroaching silence that seemed stronger than steel. Tiny broke it with his words. "You can still go home. Just let her go and move on the best you can." He smiled, almost hopeful. "It ain't too late for it."

"I fear it is." Deke said as he pulled open the door and started back inside. "Thanks, Tiny. I'll see you around." The door clunked shut, leaving Tiny alone.

"Might," Tiny whispered as he descended the steps and ambled back to his truck, the groans from the trailer swirling about him like phantoms. "Quiet," Tiny growled smacking the side of the trailer. The bang of his fist echoed through the air and the moaning faded with it. Tiny pulled himself up and in and the engine fired to life. He thumbed the tape in the deck and as Red Sovine's voice filled the cab, he put it in gear and swung out of the lot, engine sounding like the bellow of some ancient monster. In his mind, he regretted getting this all started, regretted saying anything to Deke but most of all wishing he had never said "might." Were he given the chance to end the conversation again, he would have said "I hope."

Those years with Lucille were as rich as gravy and tasted as good. Deke played them in his head as he ate up the miles and was hypnotized by the highway lines.

Lucille slipped the check under the edge of his plate as he laid his silverware on top of the dirty napkin. "I'll take that when you're ready, shy boy." she whispered and leaned back to replace the coffee pot on its warmer.

"Thanks. When do you get off?" he responded, instantly embarrassed at his lamely forward and sorely unoriginal line.

"I'm actually taking my lunch as soon as I ring you out." She stood and watched him slide a ten out of the wallet chained to his belt. He studied her smile again, wishing he had semesters to do so.

"Would you like to take a walk?" he spoke, surprising even himself.

She smiled bigger, broader and her eyes brightened.

He shrugged a little and said, "I'm about to climb up in that rig and spend another eight hours on my duff. I'd like to walk a bit while I can." He grinned and it felt like an uncomfortable shirt, tight and itchy. "Besides, I ought to walk off some of that food before I ruin this figure."

She held up a finger and walked to the register at the end of the counter. Deke looked around the place, his cheeks hot and not doubt as red as a baboon's ass. The joint was empty save for the trio of old timers at the corner booth, telling stories and slugging coffee. He stared over them and out the window, thousands of mosquitoes and gnats killing themselves.

He was drawn back to reality when she grasped his hand, gently and peeled thick fingers back to snuggle his change into his palm.

"I'd love to." she said. She did not remove her hand from his. His chest hurt, he hoped it was a heart attack, one he'd survive and experience for the rest of his life. He never gave much thought to love at first sight but damned if this wasn't it. He stood and they held their arms over the counter as they walked to the end, separated by Formica and chrome.

"Kurtzy! I'm on lunch!" Lucille hollered through the service window, her voice taking on a husky timber that was completely off from her normal sugary tone.

"Whatever! Be back in thirty!" came the seemingly disembodied bark from the kitchen, punctuated with the dropping of a pan and a few curses.

"Sure thing." she said.

Deke and Lucille stepped out into the night and the beginning of one of those loves that you only see in movies.

The night ate his smoke like squid ink disappearing in a blackened sea. He turned the stereo up a little and listened as The Possum serenaded him. Underneath the flannel and the ratty T-shirt, his belly growled, a starved dog. He sighed and scanned the horizon for the neon bright promise of future but inevitable indigestion. The night went on and on and on. The run had been a short one, three hours down and he was two hours into the return three. He felt like he hadn't eaten in days. He felt the hunger deep and wasn't so sure that it was only for food. He gripped the wheel and pushed his boot down and the night evaporated in five-thousand-two-hundred and eighty foot increments, an ounce of his soul with every one.

SIX

The new alarm clock rang at noon and Deke ignored it like a liar's promise. The almost-nasal buzzing filled the back room of the trailer like some robotic bumblebee trapped in a bucket. Deke lay in the darkness and stared at the ceiling, his left hand absently stroking the patch… the stain on the mattress.

"Morning, Love," he sighed and swung his legs around and off the bed. The thud of his boots on the floor reminded him that he'd gone to sleep in his clothes yet again.

"You're a pig, Deke," he scolded as he stood and peeled off the flannel, dropping it to the floor to cavort with the others. He made his way to the kitchen and had a hearty breakfast of toasted stale bread and instant coffee. While waiting for the water to boil, he ate a few sticks of dry spaghetti, he had no idea why. He sat down on the cases of soup and ran his hands through his greasy hair.

"You need to shower. You're a stinking fuck." He smiled and went on.

"Get some clean clothes on and get this pony show on the road." His stomach was a knotted jumble of quiver and nerves, a globe of slippery eels. He had a sense of unease that felt like the leaded apron draped over an X-ray patient. He closed his eyes and replayed the evening he came home to find his wife dead and his future hobbled.

Lucille was lying on their bed, almost. Her lower body angled in towards Deke's side, while her torso tilted over the edge toward where he stood. Her shoulders and head and one arm hung towards the floor. Her hair, that beautiful hair was swept over her slippers like a small animal. Its usually light brown sheen was darkened by the blood that was now clotting in it. Her eyes were closed, thankfully, and Deke had a suspicion one of the cops had probably done it. He breathed in heavily though his nose. The room smelled like Zippo lighter wheels and pennies. Copper and copper and copper. Blood, he knew what the fuck it was. He stepped closer and knelt.

"Please don't touch..." was all the deputy by the window got free from his mouth before Deke crippled him with a glare, a tear soaked glare that made the cop gasp.

"Out," was all Deke had to say and the man was gone, like he'd been vaporized. Deke leaned in and looked at his wife. The reason he wasn't in jail or dead by this point in his life. His angel. His anchor. Her skin was like ceramic that had been touched with a red tipped brush here and there. The blood didn't splatter or spray so much as it flowed. From her neck to the floor, some soaking into the mattress on the edge and side. A deep sob shook the man kneeling there. Tears and snot shined in his mustache and beard like tragic jewels.

He very lightly touched her cheek and looked at the knives in her throat. A pair of steak knives jutted from there like Frankenstein bolts. A little cough broke the screaming silence that was eating him alive.

"The neighbor's called it in." He wiped a finger across livery lips. "Maggie says she came over to see if Lucille wanted to have some late dinner with her and Lloyd." Deke never broke his gaze at the turned-off television. "Lucille didn't answer and when Maggie went to knock again she noticed the slit in the screen. She saw the door was open a crack and when Lucille didn't answer to her calls, she came in." He paused a few minutes, watching the man with nothing left in his world fall apart like a broken plate.

"The coroner ruled out suicide, Mr. Larch. I know it's not like she coulda done that to herself but that's procedure. They cross that off first."

The sheriff stepped into the room, "He left almost as soon as he got here, got a call about that accident out on Cromwell Road."

Deke turned and his stare latched onto the man like a lamprey.

"What?" was all he managed to say.

MacLeod took a drag on his Camel, "You heard me right. We already looked for any prints on the knives or the door and whoever did it wore gloves. There was none." The sheriff paused, "No meddling with her, the bastard who did it just broke in, killed her and left. Doesn't seem like they stole anything. Just random and senseless."

Deke looked at his wife once more, it was like looking through a windshield in the rain.

"Your boss, Mr. Boyer, took the call when we tried to contact you at work. Verified that you were on the road, on your way back at that very moment. He said he'd be able to provide manifests and shit to confirm that." The sheriff licked his lips before continuing, "You'd have been our number one suspect otherwise."

Deke didn't bother to turn; it was as though the sheriff were a shadow on the shithouse wall. Deke touched her hair and almost dared this man to say something else, anything else. He leaned over and kissed her lips. They tasted like her chap stick and a little like steak. He closed his eyes and his lips trembled against hers.

"My god," he whispered and cried into her mouth. He hoped she could swallow his pain and know it was love. It was everything he had left to give. He hoped she knew that.

When the county men arrived to take her away, Deke sat on the couch in the living room and listened as they put the love of his life in a giant bag. Watched without seeing as they loaded her on a stretcher and carried her out of his life, their life. Before he left, the sheriff had knelt beside him and stuck a couple of pills into his palm.

"Take these and close your eyes. Sleep will not come but maybe a little rest." He tried to smile but it was broken. Deke took them and nodded weakly. "I'll be by tomorrow to get some information and to take you to the parlor to make your arrangements." The older man gave Deke's hand a slight squeeze and Deke knew the man had been down this road before, perhaps many times. "Rest, Son." Sheriff MacLeod whispered and slipped out the door. And just like that, he was alone. The place was so quiet, when the valium hit the floor, it echoed.

The pot gurgled letting him know the water was hot enough and his eyes shot open like cartoon blinds. He stood and grabbed the pot with a towel.

"You can just stay home. You could call Boyer and tell him you're done and then just go shovel shit at the fertilizer plant in Craghaven." He scraped a fleck of toasted mold off the crust of his bread and took a bite. "But you gotta find out what happened. You know she didn't kill herself. You know someone came in here and did it. Tiny wouldn't shit you." He was talking to himself with a full mouth. Rude. "You can always pull out if you don't like where the trails leading." He nodded and took a swig from the dirty mug of coffee. It was atrocious. He forced the grimace up and into a smile and looked at the picture of Lucille on the table before him. He closed his eyes and left the smile on his face. He finished the rest of the vile and bitter coffee and disappeared back the hallway.

The hub was quite quiet, compared to a normal night. Only Smitty was in the Round, as they called it. The windows of Boyer's roost were suspiciously dark. Deke leaned back out the door and flicked his butt into the lot.

"Heya Smitty." he said upon re-entry. Smitty raised his hook in a solemn wave, eyes never leaving the Zane Grey in his good hand. Deke pointed up the steps, "Boyer gone for the day?"

The disbelief was barely masked. Smitty pursed blueish lips and laid the book down, pages spread like a birds wings. If Deke's pap were alive to see that he'd have smacked the man, "*Ain't no way to treat a book!*" he would have been hollering. Deke smiled and waited for Smitty to speak.

"Got one of his headaches. Turned the lights off and locked his door about two hours ago. Either sleepin' or dead. I ain't been moved to go check which yet." He leaned forward and spit in the Folger's can that sat by his desk. This, too, reminded Deke of his dear dead pappy. He grimaced and asked for his papers. Smitty reached behind the cabinet and took the clipboard from the nail. Deke felt his heart race when he saw the envelope under the clip. A dark blocky print on the front spelled out his name.

"That from Tiny?" he asked, trying to be casual. Smitty frowned at him, a frown that meant "*You know better, Boy.*" A frown that made Deke rethink this whole thing in the few seconds before the clipboard slid into his hand. Then Deke watched as the frown bent upwards into a smirk that screamed "*You definitely shoulda known better.*"

Without another word, Smitty limped back the hall to the shitter.

"Leave the clipboard, Deke," he hollered back over his shoulder as the shadows devoured him. Deke took the envelope and the sheaf of papers beneath it and laid the clipboard on the desk then went outside and to get the whole mess really started.

SEVEN

The glue on the envelope was stringy, like how your lips get after you've been sick with a cold and sleeping a while, you pull them apart and they pull and threads of dried spit and snot gum them together, that's what opening the envelope was like. Deke sat on the rotted side steps of the Cromwell Gospel House Church. It was the first house of worship he came to and even though it had not seen a service (or any sort of caretaking services) in nearly a decade, it fit the bill. Deke stole a glance at his rig, sitting over in the small gravel parking area by the overgrown graveyard. The stones jutted from the weeds like errant teeth. The paper whispered as he slid it from the envelope, a whiff of old cigar and wood smoke along with it. He opened it and looked at the pages in the feeble light cast from the pole. No doubt, it was the only thing the township bothered with maintaining. He looked over his shoulder at the faded siding and the stained glass windows. The panels broken by storm or vandal. The gutters choked with grass and nests that saw generations of birds fly away. At the simple letterboard sign that let the world know that Pastor Hendrickson presided over this house of the Lord, or had. He scooched back on the step and felt the damp on his ass from the moss that lived there. "Yuck," he groaned and shook his head. He went back to the pages.

It was a list. A literal list of almost addresses and near names. They were mythological titles accompanied by childish sketches. He studied them and shook his head. "What the hell is this shit?" he grumbled and then sheepishly added, "Sorry, Lord," as he remembered his location. He looked again at the first thing on the list, folded the paper and stuffed it into his vest pocket. He walked towards the truck, his taller shadow struggling to keep up. The sun dipped behind the trees on its way to the other side of the world and soon Deke disappeared into the fresh wound of night.

II. The Spin:

"Now who can tell what the devil does when he walks on haunted ground..." —James Hand

EIGHT

Cyclops, it had said. Written in a long webby scrawl like his Granny used to write in her Bible with. That ancient word, Cyclops and few dashes and a small circular head with one eye drawn in the middle over a "Have a Nice Day" style smile, then Rise & Shine Diner. That was it. Deke stared ahead as his truck ate up the road. "In the kingdom of the blind." he mumbled and thumbed the tape into the deck. Within a minute the cab was filled with Patsy Cline's sultry voice. Lucille's tape from when she'd ride along. Deke was hardly aware he was crying by the time he saw the diner up ahead on the right, it wasn't until he hit the wipers and they did nothing that he realized the rain wasn't outside at all. He wiped his eyes with a calloused thumb and slowed as he pulled into the diner's lot and put his head down. When the tears had stopped and dried and he was sure they'd stay away, he stepped down from the cab and headed for the diner.

The string of bells tied to the door clanged when he entered. Deke frowned a little at their loudness but walked to the counter and hopped onto one of the waiting stools. He cased the joint and his brow furrowed. There was no one here. Not a soul besides him and the two waitresses. They paid him little mind as they scuttled back and forth from the kitchen with trays of food, steaming orders that disappeared as soon as they sat them on tables. The women smiled and talked to no one and went on as though this was normal. The sound of clinking plates and silverware was almost deafening. Deke clenched his teeth and raised a hand to get the attention of one of the girls when they passed by his perch again. "What?" she said, curtly.

"I'm—" was all he got out before she jerked a thumb back to the kitchen and frowned back at him. He stood, unsurely and she repeated the gesture. "Thanks," he said before going around to the back of the counter and through the silver doors with the galley windows. He stopped and watched the two cooks scurry and pirouette around one another while frying, simmering, scalding and stirring whatever they were cooking. Getting it from griddle to plate to service window for the girls to ferry out so it could disappear at the tables. The confusion was rooting in his neck and beginning to ache. Deke was about to call to one of the cooks when a voice came from the corner behind him.

"You Deke?"

Deke spun on his heel and saw the little guy huddled over the sinks, elbows invisible beneath the mountains of soap suds that sprang from the basins.

"I am," Deke said as he took another step closer to the dishwasher. The man stopped and shook the water and soap from his arms and then dried them on the soggy apron he was wearing. He then turned and held out a damp hand in greeting.

"I'm Mike, Mike Bardo. They call me Sudsy, partly because I do dishes and partly because they're a bunch of creative fucks." He smiled. The corners of his lips seeming to touch the corners of his eyes, or eye. His left one was missing. The lids were puckered closed like a dried piece of fruit, but not completely. A sliver of darkness let you know of the void that lived behind the flesh. Mike looked around to the cooks and then at the door behind him, "Let's step into my office for this, 'kay?"

The air was chilled and the lot completely empty, save for Deke's rig, which guarded the back row like a Tolkienian beast.

"Before we get to it, I'll answer the question I know you wanna ask." Mike smiled again. He had removed his damp white work shirt, exposing a grey shirt that had most likely been black once, with the faded face of Santa Claus wearing a gas mask on the front. "You wanna know what this place is? Why the cooks are cooking' and the bitches servin' but you don't see anyone eating? Am I right?" Deke could only nod. "Because we're in the wrinkle, Brother." Mike jumped up on a stack of crates and kicked his legs like a little kid. "The people, the customers. They're on your side of the wrinkle. Real time. Us, the staff, we got the shit end of the stick. The other side of it."

Deke attempted to make some sort of sense of it, "So it isn't real? The food and all is a trick?"

"Fuck no! There is no chicanery when it comes to Ralph's cheese steaks or Tommy's fried bologna sandwiches. Bite your tongue." That smile again. "It's real. Just not on the same level as you, as we are currently." He sighed and cracked his neck. "I could lay it out all sciencey and super nerd but I'm tired. So I'm just gonna say it's like *A Wrinkle In Time*. You've read that right?"

"In sixth grade I think, I don't remember much of it," Deke replied.

"How about *Slaughterhouse-Five*?"

"Yeah, but I don't remember much of that either. "

"I remember every aspect of every thing I have ever read. Dr. Seuss to Camus to Bradbury… etcetera. I am a living encyclofuckingpedia."

Deke just stood and gaped. Sudsy just kept smiling.

"So shall we do this thing?"

Deke nodded.

"Here's the nitty gritty, I get my eye on and you ask your questions, I'll give you three. I then see what I can and answer them as I can. You don't get to badger, argue or fight over them. As is, Pal. I can't decipher, define or decode." Mike pulled a small black pouch from his shirt pocket and dug two fingers into it. "Clear?" He served up the question with a side of that fucking smile.

"As crystal." Deke said with more attitude than intended.

"Very well." he removed his fingers from the pouch, his eyes on Deke the entire time, and the item inside disappeared into his fist. He held the little sack up to his nose and sniffed. "This came with little pieces of gum, supposed to look like gold nuggets. I swallowed it all and didn't shit for days. Still smells like it. Smells like the gum, not the delayed shit." Sitting in his palm was an old ten-sided die, the kind they used in those *Dungeons & Dragons* games. It was bright red. Mike held it out to Deke, "Take it and shake it. Then drop it back into my hand."

Deke took it and hesitated. It felt odd in his hands. Warm and soft like flesh or river clay in June. He did as he was told and shook it vigorously before dropping it back into Mike's waiting hand. Without looking at it Mike slammed his hand against his empty eye socket. There was a noise much like the scrunch of bubble wrap before he opened the lid. The number seven showed. Mike gasped sharply and his breath was appeared like a ghost. "Ask," he said. There were no smiles, not anymore.

Deke stared at the starless sky. There had been stars moments ago, hadn't there? He looked at Mike as he panted tiny tufts of breath into the darkness. "Who killed Lucille?" he asked, his words coins in a tin pail. He stitched "That's all I need to know," onto the end of the query. The question hung there, almost visible.

Mike rocked back and forth, muttering indecipherable words and huffing chilled breath into the air. Deke hugged himself tight in the new cold. He sniffed, the icy air seizing his sinuses. He wished he had a cigarette.

"I see a hand on the screen door. Thick fingers like links of sausage. Black and shiny." Mike spoke in a deadpan drone, an old recording full of pop and hiss. "I see it clench and cough out a blade. I see a blade kiss the screen and slice a hole like a mouth. Fist punches through and grips the knob. One turn and the world catches fire." Mike kept his hand over the good eye. Deke leaned on every word. "The knob turns and he enters. There is the sound of a television coming out the hall. Voices followed by fake laughter. One Day At A Time. He walks along the wall, cloaked in the shadow, he is close to invisible."

Mike stopped speaking. A tear dribbled from the corner of his eye socket. It was bloody. Mike sniffed and his bottom lip trembled.

"It was you." He abruptly plucked the die from his head with a wet slurp. He jammed it into his shirt pocket and stood. "It's been real," he said, wiping the palms of his hands on his damp jeans and forcing a smile and a chuckle. Both were unconvincing. He turned and made for the door.

"Stop," Deke said, calm but stern.

"You asked. I answered. We're done, unless you got two more questions I said I'd tackle three." Mike shrugged and sidestepped towards the door.

Deke held up a hand in a gesture of near panic. "I ain't gonna hurt you. I never hurt anyone, in my life. Well, outside of a couple of bar fights but that don't count. I never killed not a one." Deke stepped closer to the young man and he backed up as well. "I wasn't even there. I was on the road when she died. I just got home from a run after she was killed." Deke's voice cracked. "I swear," he added.

Mike rested his hand on the edge of the dumpster. Behind him the door opened a crack and a voice mumbled something low.

"God forbid one of you fucks washes some glasses!" Mike yelled inside. His attention returned to Deke, who was now sitting on the ground sobbing quietly. "Look. I just say what I see. It isn't always a literal thing. Not always. Sometimes it's like symbolism. Sometimes it's not. Might be that it isn't really you…but was because of you." He stopped and looked around. "That isn't much better though, is it?"

Deke remained silent. Mike stepped back and stuck out his hand to the man, fighting the uncomfortable smile trying to worm onto his pale face. Deke took it and rose, shakily.

"Again, it might be not as I saw it. I can only say what I saw. Note it and keep digging. And hopefully, It's more than that… better than that. Shit, I never know what to say." Mike chewed on his thumbnail.

Deke patted him on the shoulder. "Thanks for looking. Better get in there and wash them dishes. I'll take a rain check on them other two questions." With that Deke walked to his truck and climbed inside, a Jonah disappearing into the mouth of the whale.

NINE

Deke's rig clicked as the engine cooled in the night air. It sat in the far corner of the parking lot of the Deagle Line rest stop. The vague glow from the street lights almost reached the faded paint and bug-clotted grill. The truck awaited its master like some great mythological beast. The rest area was quiet save for the occasional whoosh of a vehicle whizzing by on the highway.

Deke stood over the toilet for what seemed like an hour. The floating urine froth reminded him of the eyes of a spider, staring through him. He leaned forward and felt the cool tile of the wall press against his forehead. He thought he could almost hear the sizzle of his hot skin touching the cold ceramic. He closed his eyes and another tear cascaded down his stubbled cheek. Out in the main part of the restroom, the door banged open and someone shuffled to one of the urinals. Piss hissed as it hit and the culprit let out a rapturous sigh. They were just two men ridding themselves of salt water.

TEN

"Remember the ashes under your tongue?" The voice sounded like the feel of a dead fish. Deke nodded in the darkness. "What of your father's kisses or your mother's upon the lid of each eye at bed time? The unspoken volumes in each?" Deke tried to open an eye—then both—but the lids were tiny anvils.

"Yes." came his weak reply, a frail thing on a dank breeze. It felt like a lie.

"The fires, the seas and the sky—what a ménage a trois?" the other voice continued, each word dipped in honey and drain water, sweet and vile at the same time. Daddy long legs scurried over each syllable.

"Yeah," Deke grunted, his head spinning in the shadows. He smelled gasoline and rubber and wet cloth. A dull thrum pulsed behind his eyes. His head was killing him.

Something wispy touched his wrist and then his cheek. He hoped it was just hair or a cobweb. It lingered like the voice. Then it occurred to him that these words were familiar, like slipping your hand into a worn leather glove that had been boxed up since last winter. He thought hard, wiggling mental fingers to loosen the stiff hide but this achieved nothing but more throbbing in his temples. He was sure he could hear smiling.

There was a cough followed by a noise that sounded like a hammer hitting steak. The speaker's tongue wetted his lips: "You'd do better to forget them."

Fingers touched his face, pulling the blindfold up and over his head. Then the trunk of the car slammed closed. One dark place traded for another.

Outside, in the night above, planets died grisly deaths or withered away while the cosmos swirled. Underneath it all it was just as black as where Deke Larch entered fitful sleep.

ELEVEN

The light was a blazing hammer in the face. Deke sat up and froze like one of those thousand legged insects that scurry up water pipes and bathroom walls only to freeze when you turn on the light, becoming Frankenstein scars on tile. Every joint ached and felt backwards. Every bone in his body seeming to pop or crack in dispute. He peered through the film of bug guts and dirt and surmised he was in the truck, in the parking lot of the Hub. It was empty save for his rig. He pressed his fingers into his eyes until spots danced and then sniffed hard enough to make his sinuses burn. He slid over to the driver's side and opened the door. When his feet hit the concrete it shook him. He felt like a man made of plastic baggies, filled with broken candy canes. All sharp points, glassy angles and minty tingle. He plodded toward the building, his muscles nagging and bitching all the way.

The door felt like it was made of brick; it took both hands to push it open. Why was he so weak today?

Deke groaned quietly and regarded Smitty's desk. A sheaf of papers on a taped up clipboard, a mug full of pens and pencils, his nekkid lady calendar. Smitty's spit can sitting on the floor between the desk and the filing cabinet. A giant horsefly buzzed as it tried to extract itself from the acrid sludge in the can, like a tiny dinosaur trying to get out of a tar pit. No Smitty. "Probably in the shitter," he said to no one and made his way over to the battered sofa along the wall. He leaned back and rested his head on the lumpy cushion.

He worked the pages of Tiny's letter from his back pocket and unfolded them. The second page had one word across the top, *Behemoth*. Under the word was a scrawled doodle of what looked like a blob with a little head on top. It wore a smiley face.

#1476 Kenwood Valley Road was written underneath it. Deke sighed through his nose and refolded the letter, sliding it into the chest pocket of his flannel. He closed his eyes and was asleep in seconds, this time with no dreams at all.

TWELVE

Deke approached the building. It looked as though it had once been a small garage, just two bays attached to the little office part. Dirt and grime coated all of the windows. The filth, punctuated with dead wasps and spiders. Cobwebs draped everywhere. The list shook in his hand a little as he checked the address against the numeric stickers on the door frame. One. Four. Seven. The curled remains of the six rested in a pile of soggy and rotting newspapers. "This is the place." he mumbled and strode to the door. There was a chain looped through the handle but no lock. He untangled the links and dropped the chain to the ground with a Jacob Marley timbre of clanking. He entered the small room. His face instantly shriveled… that smell. He slung an arm over his nose and kicked an old oil can between the door and the jamb to keep it open, a feeble attempt to allow some air in and that foul air out.

Under a large cracked window, buried under a pile invoices that looked like parchment, was a desk. Decades of sunlight through dirty glass had bleached the paper to dead skin scrolls. On the corner, there was an ashtray that was overflowing, the foundation of a miniature mountain of ash and filter. A candy machine flanked the side wall; the candy had been long ago poached by mice and roaches. Shreds of wrappers and shit coated the coils and glass. Deke coughed and stepped towards the door that led to the first bay. He hesitated and considered the list again and shook his head. He was terrified at what the "Behemoth" might be. He pulled the door open and the stench flooded over him like a sour wave.

He remained rooted in the doorway. He simply could not move. The floor of the bay was covered with a tarpaulin, probably more than one. Blue and faded where it showed, that is. Most of it was smothered by flesh.

The Behemoth was a man, maybe. More accurately he was a thousand pound puddle of flesh. A rippling mound of flab and skin, his feet no longer visible beneath their cloaking pouches of bruise colored tissue. Cascades of bright and angry pimples formed constellations. Wounds oozed where the skin simply could not hold any longer. His pendulous breasts hung over his gut. Nipples jutted like extra thumbs. His arms had no choice but to stick straight out; the copious amounts of fat kept him from putting them down. The hair beneath them was dreadlocked with fetid clots of dried sweat and who knew what else.

His head was freakishly small, because it was a normal sized head cradled in a deep waddle of skin and fat. His eyes bulged and watered. His chin was slick with drool, and judging from the welty redness of the flesh there, it always was.

Deke could do nothing but stare. His own eyes watering as well, due to the odious assault of sweat and a cheesy fermentative stench, excrement and salty ammonia, which attacked his senses. Flies bounced through the air, lazy and large as bumblebees.

"You a shy boy?" the fat man wheezed. There was a small giggle from the far corner, where the light barely reached.

Deke looked there and saw the little man on the chair. Short and skinny and dressed in a jumpsuit that had possibly been blue once but was now bilge water drab. The man sat with knees under chin and watched Deke intently. He was drawn up like a cat about to pounce.

"Not shy. A little shocked," Deke said.

The fat man laughed, it was the sound of meat sizzling in a skillet. Deke imagined it probably smelled like that too. The laughter turned into a ragged cough and the little man popped from his seat, simian quick and scaled the expanse of the fat man's chest with nimble speed. He carried a water bottle in hand and a long straw for the man-puddle to drink through. The bottle was emptied in a blink and the little man was back on his perch just as fast.

The fat man wiggled and rippled, trying to raise himself enough to take in Deke. The walls shook slightly and Deke could see the bright blue of the tarp where it had been protected from light and air by the tonnage of flesh that obscured it. The smell grew thicker, Deke held his breath.

"I know you," the words oozed from the fat man's lips. Slowly and wetly rolling over them like little lettery worms. Deke winced and shook his head. Heat radiated from the mass of the man, sweat beaded on Deke's forehead.

"I ain't never met you," he replied. "I damn sure would've remembered that."

The fat man smiled. It was cold and sharp like a razor wound, the only element of the man that carried angles. "I didn't say I knew you this time 'round. We get on this ride many times, brother. Funny thing that." He paused and began gulping air, creating a wet and slapping sound like children in a wading pool.

"You'd think we'd learn from our fuck ups but we really just put on a new suit and walk the same tracks in the same yellow snow. Follow the same scent trails and die in the same traps." There was a pause filled with labored wheezes-a dying accordion.

"Sin stinks-has a smell and reek. Every person is different; it's like a signature. We change skins and names but that smell is the same. Always. Like changing clothes and wetting your hair instead of actually washing-you look proper but smell like Hell." That smile again, wider than possible. How many teeth did this man have and why were they all so little and sharp?

"And you, Sir, smell like Hell."

Something squealed in the corner, or maybe in Deke's chest.

After a fit of gagging that nearly cause him to pass out, Deke said, "I'm looking for someone." The fat man grinned at him, a one-ton Cheshire cat. A cockroach scurried across his stomach where it disappeared like a stone being thrown into a well. Deke could have sworn the man's bellybutton chewed. Deke closed his eyes and swallowed hard, heard the crunch of carapace and the wheezing of the man's breath.

"We all are," the fat man spoke. A thin reedy fart punctuated his statement.

"I want to find the man who killed my wife. It's that simple," Deke said, in a rapid burst of words, hoping to say it before he had to taste the stink of the room. He pushed a fist to his lips and held it there. The fat man bent his small arms inward, as much as possible.

"Simple is a myth, carried in a basket by gods and imbeciles," the fat man giggled. It was the sound of burbling water in a sewer drain.

His fingers began to elongate, like something from a horror movie. Skeletal and talon-like. They stretched and stretched. The little man in the corner giggled again. Deke watched, struck dumb by it all.

"I'm a sin-eater," the Behemoth spoke. "My family always have been. I however, developed what you might call an eating disorder." He laughed and it was a skinless creature being thrown against the bricks. "I started out the usual way, the bereaved would place their dead upon the table. Cover the corpse with fruits and vegetables and succulent meats." The drool seemed to thicken and foam on the fat man's waddle. "The food absorbs the sin and we eat it, clearing the slate for the dead to move on."

Deke averted his eyes, staring at the fly strips that hung from the ceiling. They were heavy with flies and mosquitoes like bunches of strange fruit

"One day, I found I didn't need it. The food as a medium. I was standing next to a man at the station. I began to drool. I felt my stomach warm and my head began to flood with visions. I saw and tasted him punching his wife in the side of the head for burning his breakfast. I savored the flavor of theft of every dollar embezzled from his employer. I stood and glutted on this man's baleful misery and sin. And by the time we got on the bus, I was quite full. And bigger. I'd popped the button of my trousers." At this, the man chortled once more. "That was when I wore clothes. Such an overrated commodity. A waste in many respects. Anyway... And so it went. I could siphon sin from anyone I was near. And I grew. Oh, how I grew. One who feeds on misery is never at a loss for a meal, you know." That smile was basin wide and full of more teeth than possible. The Behemoth stopped laughing suddenly. "I can also recall every single metaphysical meal. Every psychic succulence." His eyes twinkled and those overlong fingers began to caress his girth, almost disgustingly sexual, the tips delving into the rolls and folds.

"Here is a fellow named Bartlett. Nice enough man but he worked in areas best left untouched. His sin tasted of clove and anise. He was merely a snack compared to some." Another burst of moist laughter and then right back to seriousness.

"You know, preachers and politicians are a feast in and of themselves. I used to love church socials and campaign trails. Veritable smorgasbords."

The little man was standing on the chair now, leaning towards a fly strip that dangled above his head. He reached out and plucked a dead fly from it and popped it into his mouth. All at once, the buzzing and scurrying of vermin and bugs ceased.

The room became a vault. Not a sound.

"About you," the fat man said, his voiced echoing in the bay. "How tasty, you were." The little man tittered in the corner and Deke's head went light as a feather before going heavy as a cinder block. He fell to the floor.

Deke opened his eyes and looked into the ferrety face of the little man. He waved his hands and the man scurried back to his corner seat. Deke pulled himself up on his knees and shook his head a little.

"Being confronted by your own wrongs is heavy business," the fat man said. "Like being smacked with a pillowcase full of stones." Deke nodded and tried to recall all that had been said. "You know, Brother Larch, that not sinning is the worst sin of all?" He paused and licked those liver-like lips. "Unused potential is waste and waste is a sin, Apathy is a sin. Contentment is a sin." The rhythm of the Behemoth's speech was like a locomotive gaining steam. "Refusal to change is a sin. Letting love die in your grasp is a sin." The cadence revved, increasing in speed. "Complacency is a sin. Acceptance is a sin." And then like a terrible wreck it all stopped. The room and all sound in it became a vacuum and the obese man stared at Deke his smile growing like cancer. "Deke Larch is a sin."

With that, the blob closed his eyes. The little man wrung out the mildewed towel soaking in a pail. He climbed up the man's chest and laid the towel over the Behemoth's reddened face. The small man looked at Deke and shook his head. Deke lowered his and left the room and its gangrenous reek. Outside, night had lumbered in and clubbed the day to death, like a neanderthal.

III: The Slide

*"Dread the darkness, hate the daylight.
Sorrow breaks a good man down"*
—Waylon Jennings

THIRTEEN

Deke sat in the truck and gazed out at the cemetery. His Pap had always called them "bone gardens." The morning mist rose in finger curls from the crisp grass. The leaves were starting to change on the trees and a few early suicides littered the ground. With a heavy sigh, he opened the door and hopped down. He walked four rows down and three rows over, stopping under the gnarled claw of a small tree. He dropped to his knees and the cold dew soaked through the denim. He touched the stone before him , tracing the L and the U with calloused fingertips. His lip began to quiver and his eyes welled. He had put off this visit for months. He knelt for about twenty minutes talking to his wife.

    He had called his Dad to tell him he was in love, one of the few times he called. He heard that gruffly sweet "Hello," and started jabbering across the miles of wire. He told everyone and anyone who would give a minute about this stunning creature that had stolen his heart. "When she looks at me and smiles. I look at the ground. My heart is as thin as a dime but I'd give it to her anyway. In her small hand, it would look like a doubloon. She could cram it in the slot in my back and see all the senseless tricks I would perform, to make her smile again." The man at the bank drive-thru window had just gawped at him. Deke smiled and took his envelope of money and drove home.

They married eight months later, in the Justice's office in a small town called Ochseville in the mountainous wilds of Pennsylvania. The town was a pimple on the neck that was the run through the coal regions, almost smack dab between Harrisburg and Pittsburgh. By that time, Lucille had quit the diner and was riding with Deke for the long hauls and setting up a home in the ramshackle trailer he had already owned, and ignored, for a few years. She would wash his filthy road jeans and shirts and she helped him clean his truck. They took long walks around the park, chatted with neighbors. They held hands and smiled at one another, always, with eyes and mouths. She earned some extra money working as a math tutor, a job choice that made gooseflesh sprout on Deke's hairy neck. Math was of the Devil, he always said and faked a shiver. They'd laugh and usually end up in each others arms. They had started talking about the B word about two weeks before she was killed.

"You oughta let me cut them weeds," the voice behind him advised. Deke stood and turned to face the man. The stern frown that had crouched to attack melted instantly. Deke smiled and let the tears keep running.

"Doyle," he said and hugged his cousin, clapping the man on the shoulder.

Doyle smiled his simple smile and repeated himself.

"Lucille's bed is growed up with weeds. Ought to let me cut 'em back." Deke shook his head and looked down at the grave. "I'd be happy to," the man continued.

Dandelions and nameless weeds fought for space at the base of the stone. Dead flowers lay around them like fallen soldiers.

"I think graves oughta be a little bit untidy, like lives are." Doyle nodded and wiped at his nose with the faded handkerchief in his big hands.

"Want some coffee?" Deke smiled and shook his head. "You can see the baby, if she ain't sleepin'," Doyle added. He turned and made steps toward the cottage.

Deke stopped and felt a dozen shivers run up and down his spine. His smile dipped and drowned within him.

"No thanks, cuz. I gotta get going. I have a run today."

Doyle turned and raised a hand. "I know. Be careful. Maybe you can stop by for dinner some day?" was all he said. This time there was no smile on his moonish face, all the sadness there allowed no room for it. Deke went back to his truck. Before getting in, he turned and watched his cousin open the door and go inside. From the open window, a baby's cries floated on the mist.

He hated seeing babies now. Hearing them was almost worse. Deke had always wanted kids, but never wanted to be a dad who wasn't there. His own father had walked out when Deke was seven and the rest of their relationship had endured strains and pains as a result. By the time they had actually started to repair the bridge that was their father and son bond, fate stepped in. And fate being the bastard it is, poured a liberal dose of fucking cancer on his old man and that was that. Regret is a sour thing, a thing you can never fully swallow or cough up but something shitty that dances and dangles at the back of your throat causing nothing but misery and annoyance. Deke didn't want history to repeat itself as history is wont to do. But they had been discussing it. Had been. He could fill a trailer or two with all of the fucking had beens.

Deke turned the key and was happy that the engine blotted out all other sound.

FOURTEEN

The water was starting to boil as he broke the handful of dry spaghetti in half and then in half again. He dropped the pasta into the water and stirred it around a little, watching it froth a bit as he did so. He opened the cupboard, shook his head and turned to the fridge. He got out a half stick of butter, a bottle of hot sauce and half an onion that was beginning to sprout. He walked over to the table and dug into his inner coat pocket and pulled out two Slim Jims. He went back to the stove and stirred the pasta again. With a dirty knife he chopped the meat sticks into small pieces and tossed them in, then did the same with the old onion. He stirred it all until the noodles were soft. He drained the water into the sink and then threw in the butter and the rest of the hot sauce. He mixed it around until he had a panful of orange sour smelling mess. He picked up his eggy fork from breakfast and headed for the couch. He looked over at the stack of soup by the table, three cases of it, all vegetable beef, all long out of date. He kept eating his concoction, his nose running and his eyes stinging with each bite. He was sure it was going to do a number on his ass later when it made its escape. He sat the pan on top of the old newspapers that covered his coffee table. He leaned back and pushed his thumbs into his eyes as he tried to assemble the pieces of information given to him by Tiny's weirdos. He was having as much luck as he would were he putting together a thrift store puzzle. He sighed and belched loudly. The shit didn't taste any better the second time.

FIFTEEN

The run of the day was a short one, a load of air conditioners to a warehouse out near Contorville. Six hours behind the wheel gave Deke more time to be alone with his thoughts, although most of the time he'd rather be alone with a starving alligator. He pulled his rig in and parked in the trailer's drive way. He was fortunate enough to have neighbors who didn't mind looking at the diesel-swilling brontosaurus that sat among them. He killed the engine and sat a while, his brain working overtime today to sort through the slivers of information he'd gotten, or the lack thereof. He had devoured miles today, shifting and sliding things forgotten and unremembered (yes, there is a difference) as he drove, like one of those cheap plastic puzzles you got as a kid, sliding the tiles around and up or down and arrange them to complete the picture.

The Cyclops had said he was responsible. The Behemoth had basically given that foundation and gone so far as to say Deke was destined to backstroke in the lake of fire. He wasn't coming up with much beyond that and he was too tired to keep going. Deke rubbed his eyes. They burned like he'd been standing by a burning brush pile. He breathed heavily and snorted as he opened the door and bounded out. He looked over at the Wehunt's trailer. Their car was gone and there were no lights burning. He mounted the sagging steps and went inside.

Within a few minutes, Tompall was singing about "Drinking them beers," his voice floating from the dirty windows and into the dying daylight. Deke sat on the sofa and propped his feet up on the coffee table, hiding at least seven ring stains from view. He threw an arm over his eyes and sat there, resting—thinking. But a few minutes after that, he was snoring.

"Remember those ashes under your tongue?" Deke sat up quickly. He had only begun the dream, but something in his mind clamped on that line like a foot trap, the rusted teeth digging into the mental ankle bone. Maybe it wasn't surreal and symbolic, as dreams are often supposed to be. But what if this was literal instead?

He found himself thinking back to a day, a few years ago, Deke had not been with Boyer's outfit very long. Boyer had developed a serious ulcer on the underside of his tongue. He wouldn't go to the doctor but it got so bad that he couldn't eat. Deke told him of an old farm remedy, used by his great grandma. Cigar ashes. Take a pinch of ashes and put them on the ulcer and let them moisten and cake there. It burns and doesn't taste very nice but it will draw the inflammation out and the sore will heal. Boyer did it and it worked. The way he was with Deke after that, you'd have thought he removed a splinter from the man's paw. He played the dream line in his head again. "Remember the ashes under your tongue?" It troubled him that the voice speaking it sounded a lot like his.

SIXTEEN

The paper crinkled in the dim light of the cab. The word "Faun" was scribbled in leaning script and the address below was the same as where he had parked the idling truck. Below it, was Tiny's notation in pale blue ink.

"You know this one." The glow of the sign in front of the Cesare Grill barely reached the edge of the lot where he was parked. The fog ate up the light in ragged bites. Deke sighed, butted out his cigarette and turned off the engine, cutting off Milsap in mid-song. He listened as the engine died and then got out and headed for the diner. His footsteps tapped a lonely beat.

The diner was a little noisier than usual. The clank of plates on tables and the clinking of spotty forks and knives being wrapped in napkins. The sign said PLEASE WAIT TO BE SEATED and he scanned the booths as he did. Then he saw her. It had to be her but how she ended up in with this mess, he couldn't fathom. He began walking in her direction. She just sat and waved him on, pretty as spring and smiling just as big.

"Deke!" she called. He lowered his head a little as he made his way across the bustling room. It felt like pond water to hear his name called by a woman. He slid into the empty side of the booth and bumped an elbow on the table. He scowled and rubbed it as he scooched in a little more and got comfortable.

"Not funny at all, huh?" she asked, the smile still on her lips and dusting the corners of her eyes. Those eyes. Large and barely green. He almost stared but his stomach began to churn. He felt a heat blossom in his neck and he chewed the inside of his cheek for distraction.

"Been a lot of years, Kristi," he said. "Looks of things, time's been a lot kinder to you than me. You look just as pretty as you did when we were in school."

She laughed. It was throaty and true. "Well, things aren't always as they seem or so the saying goes." She slid a slender arm across the table and wriggled her middle two fingers into his closed hand.

He squinted a little and smiled broader. "You really look just as good as you did then."

"Deke, stop." Her smile returned… had it ever left? She gave his thick fingers a small squeeze. He smiled himself, but it felt as though it had shrunk in the wash.

"Let's get our orders in," he said. She nodded and lowered her head, thinking of how his hand felt strong and warm and tired from grasping at straws. She looked at the yellow tint on his fingers from the countless cigarettes held between them. Deke thought her delicate paw felt like thirty pieces of silver.

"Guess you know why I'm here, if you're on my list," He managed to say during a lull in their reminiscing, after the waitress had brought their orders. She nodded, her smile fleeing like a scared mouse. She nursed her drink. It was so quiet in the place now, he could hear her soda fizz. He looked at her, almost, finding it difficult to make eye contact. She held the cup in a shaking hand. Together, they watched the condensation bead and roll down to the bottom before suicidal leaps to the table top.

She sat down her drink and took his hand again, without wiping the wet from her fingers. "I know you've been struggling. And I know alone. It's one of the saltiest tastes. Like eating rock salt. It burns and fires thirst. A thirst you'll never kill." She stroked his finger with her thumb, feeling the thick dead skin's sandpapery rub. He felt warm and a bit dizzy. But it felt nice and welcome. He had missed contact.

"Just trying to find some answers. I miss Lucille so much, Kristi."

He paused. "I feel like a shit being here with you. Like I'm up to no good. She's gone almost two years and I still feel like I shouldn't even look at another woman. I know she was killed. I know it wasn't me. Maybe because of me, but not me." He tilted his head quickly to the left and his neck cracked sharply. "I know when I find out who did it, the world will have to split in two to hold all the blood that's coming. All the rage."

"All that anger." Kristi leaned in, her small nose almost touching his. His eyes widened. "You can't be a vessel for it, Deke. You're a good man, a kind man. You used to be. All that hate and anger is twisting you into what you aren't. Making you a scarecrow."

"What I wasn't," he corrected.

"Deke, you are a sore left to fester. Every attempt to scab and heal, you've torn away with the fidgety fingers of a child." She squeezed his hand tightly. "You've stockpiled enough guilt and anger and grief to choke an army. And when you find the person who killed her, you gotta know there is no coming back from that." He could have peeled the worry from her face with a putty knife.

"I have nothing. A man with nothing is the most dangerous beast." He drank his now flat cola in a single swig. "More dangerous than that, I am Nothing."

"You have everything, Deke. The future." She leaned back in her seat, slipping her small bird of a hand from his. He looked down at the table. His reflection in the formica. He was a statue carved of sadness and anger. A masterwork painted in heartbreak and desperation. Beautifully ugly. Across the table, however, she was just beautiful.

They picked at their food. Kristi nibbled on some cold fries and Deke ate half of his burger, only after picking off the lettuce and tomato. The silence cocooned them. Deke looked at Kristi. His brow furrowed slightly as he remembered something. He held up a spoon and dropped it on the floor. It clanged like a bell. He leaned over and down to retrieve it and he saw Kristi close her eyes and hide her face as he did so. The spoon was lying near where her feet should have been. He touched her hoof with his pinky while retrieving it.

He sat up so fast he hit his head on the table, nearly spilling her drink. His expression belied his shock and confusion. She slid her hands from her face and smiled. It was the smile of children who are nervous. "What?" was all he said, his eyes wide, "Your legs?" he added as she took his hand and leaned in close.

"I was in an accident. Not long after I dropped out of college. I was driving in the rain, in bumfuck nowhere. Somewhere down south. There was no hospital and no phones. It was like in *Misery* when Annie Wilkes is telling Sheldon about the phones lines being down and the roads being closed and all that, only in my case it was true. I was lucky—sort of—the first person to come along was a retired doctor. He became the area veterinarian. He had his partner with him, who was a taxidermist." She paused as the waitress came by to refill their drinks and ask about dessert. Deke ordered a slab of cake to buy them more time. His expression was a freshly cleaned chalkboard.

"Anyway, the doctor saved my life but ended up taking the left leg at the knee. He took the right leg a week later. I was unconscious for weeks. So I wasn't awake for any of it. I'm certain I would have protested if I was able. You know, I'm a small town girl but I know keeping a person in your house and performing major surgeries on them is more than a little fucked up." She smiled and he tried his hand at it. His was a clumsy foal.

She resumed her story: "Regardless, once I was awake and saw my legs were gone. I was bitter and angry. I wanted to die. Gunnells, that was the name of the doctor explained to me that it was foolish to spit on gifts you receive. That them coming upon me that night, at that time was the only thing that allowed me to still be breathing. I needed to count my blessings and embrace the gift I had been given. A future. He and Craig were angels, Deke. Flesh and blood helpers, here to do good. I was given a new role."

"And those?" was all Deke had to add.

"Well, Craig, the taxidermist fellow, set about making me some legs. Prosthetics so unique, they would allow me to not only walk but to show how special I was. How lucky to be walking among the world- among the world but not a part of it. I had changed or was changed. I was now something more than I could have been. It's said that tragedy leaves the deepest marks. Craig made these from the hind legs of a deer. Well, not literally, he designed them based on the deer leg concept. He used the same design for the steel skeleton and then covered that with plastics and resin or rubber and whatnot.

When that was done, he covered it all with deer hide. And put the hooves on instead of feet. They were surprisingly easy to learn to walk on. Balance is balance and you've either got it or you don't."

"That's a lot to buy. Seems a bit ridiculous. Like some mad scientist movie." Deke leaned over to look at her legs again. Her floral skirt hung like a curtain with slender back-kneed-brown-furred legs beneath.

"I realize." She smirked. "You've known me since school so I couldn't really play the *I was born this way* card, could I?"

"Guess not, although I never saw you out of jeans back then. Much as I wished." He smiled. The slightly risqué innuendo tasted like undercooked meat to him. He wasn't a fan of the flavor.

"Maybe I was abducted by aliens and this was some experiment gone awry?" She tried again and smiled bigger, accenting it with a wink.

Deke nodded.

"So after relearning to walk and finally getting back home, I began having visions. Callings, I think. I could sense things in people and places and see where the road was heading. Where my fellow beacons on the Soul Road can only suggest or advise, I can actually change things, Deke. I can offer you a solution. I can change your mind."

Deke just stared.

"It's what I do, I try."

She leaned even closer and placed her warm lips to his dry ones. She kissed him so softly and honestly that even as his tears ran down over their lips, salty and sad, she did not stop. They didn't part for a minute or two and neither one opened their eyes.

"Did that work?" she asked. Her eyes were brambles threatening to snag and snarl him fast.

He took her hand and raised it to his lips, kissing it lightly. "I'm doing this, Kristi. I'm getting answers. The clues I've gotten are starting to fall in place and I think Ill have what I need pretty soon."

"Deke. You know it isn't that easy."

"Were you put on my list just to try and talk me out of it? That seems a bit stupid."

"My job is to present the path. Show you how it is going to go. I told you that. You're going to find the one you hold responsible and you will kill that one and wrath will show itself in all that blue flamed glory. And once he is released there is no coming back. Wrath is a god of no good returns."

"I can't just close the door, Kris. I've been sitting in the howling wind, letting it burn my skin and eyes with its blistering cold. And I can't close it." He drew a breath that sounded anchor heavy. "I need it closed."

Deke hung his head low and slid to the edge of the booth, still holding her hand. "Walk with me a bit."

She slid out on her side and they left the diner. The waitress scurried by and picked up the pair of tens under the ketchup bottle. She never bothered to turn and watch the pretty girl with the legs of a deer walk out with a trucker who wore all the pain of the world on his face.

SEVENTEEN

The moon was a ragged clipped thumbnail on a black bandana. The air was warmer than it had been. Deke walked, holding Kristi's hand tightly, as though she were a balloon likely to be stolen by the breeze. She walked beside him, taking smaller strides. Her hooves clicked on the macadam. He stole a glance down at them and then looked over at her, shaking his head and laughing a little. She just smirked. A few truckers passed them enroute to greasy glory, acknowledging the couple with a nod or a smile. Deke couldn't believe that not a single person took a double take at Kristi's legs. He looked over at her and cleared his throat.

"I have a question." She interrupted him, holding up the hand that wasn't entwined with his.

"I bet I know what it is. Remember when you met with Sudsy and you saw the food and the waitresses but not the people eating stuff?" Deke stopped and nodded, his left eyebrow making an upside down V over his eye. "My legs are like that. I mean, they're really deer legs, well, false legs made to look like deer legs, but most folks can't see that. A lot of people aren't tuned to see exception. It's like that old saying about how anyone can hear but it taking a special person to listen." He shook his head once more and they walked on. Kristi squeezed his hand hard enough to crack knuckles and said, "Tell me about her."

Deke's voice was a hinge in need of oil, a desert screaming for rain and a lonely man who lost the only woman he ever needed. They stopped walking.

"She was perfect," he said. He cleared his throat, "Not really. But to me, for me, she was." He glanced sidelong. Kristi wore no expression. In fact, for a brief second her face was an egg. Just smooth and white. He blinked and she was as she had been. Big eyes, freckles across her little nose, those lips.

"We met and it was love at first sight. Like a Paul Williams song or an old movie. If we were a cartoon, little pink hearts and birds would've flown around above our heads."

Kristi laughed and pulled his arm. They resumed their stroll. "Just hearts," she corrected. "The birds are for when you get hit with a hammer or an anvil is dropped on your head."

Deke pulled her arm back. "Quiet, you!" They giggled but his smile withered quickly.

"We had a good thing going," he continued. "She was teaching math to surly teens and I was hauling and we didn't have a fortune but we made due. We were happy, I thought. She was talking about wanting to start a family." Deke's voice began to crack. "I wanted to wait a bit, I wanted to be goddamn sure. My parents split when I was little and I wanted to make sure that wasn't gonna happen to a child of mine." He stopped walking and faced the woods. He thought he heard whispers mingling with the crickets. Could have sworn he saw a white face or two flit through the tangle and growth.

"We'd had a fight. And I got my head twisted and lit out on a run. I told Boyer, I was taking the haul early and I needed to cool my head. He was fine with it, actually smiled when I took the manifest and shit." Deke heard the words as he said them, like the first time, his brow furrowing and creasing.

He paused and saw Kristi's face. She was crying and nodding. Her eyes just leaked and leaked but no sound escaped that little mouth. "He even gave me the money for a room and told me to check in and sleep after the drop off. He didn't want me driving back tired and pissed. Sleep and calm your ass down and come home tomorrow was what he said."

His words were a stuttering train of syllables, intermixed with her sniffling sobs. The puzzle in his head was clicking and clacking as his mental thumbs slid the tiles around. Deke was sitting in the empty spot, the non-tile that gives you the leeway to move the rest. The picture was almost complete.

"I think…" he choked, his eyes widening a little.

"I know. But it could very easily just be that," she mumbled and eyed the ground.

EIGHTEEN

The truck was warm. Kristi sat next to Deke in its cab, in the shotgun seat. The fur on her legs almost shimmered in the glow of the dashboard lights.

"I know," he said. The thin ribbon of snot on his upper lip disappeared with a snort. She nodded and bit her bottom lip.

"You think," she said, it was the sound of the surf at two in the morning.

He stared ahead and just kept nodding. "I'm pretty sure, I know. I've worked at it in my head and all signs seem to be pointing one way."

"Straight down," she tacked on. Deke acted as though he didn't hear her. She twisted a little to face him. "Deke. Please. You need to get your head right. Nothing you're thinking is right. Nothing is what you're seeing. It's like someone painted your glasses blue and you're still trying to read through them. All the grief and the loneliness and the anger and the guilt. All of that has eaten you to nothing." She felt her fingers working at the hem of her dress. "And the shred that was left has woven you a new body. Thatched a new you outta thorny vines and scab and barbed wire. You're a sonofabitch of loss."

"More like I'm a motherfucker of misery," he chimed in.

She paused to unleash a sob or three. "Please Deke. Just stop it. Let it go. Put your foot down and drive."

He turned to her. "I wish I could. I can't. The door's been open so long. I gotta kick that thing closed and nail the fucker shut forever." He laid his head on the steering wheel. "It has to be done," he shouted.

Kristi just watched him, "I wish you would listen. I'll stay with you if you just leave. If we just leave."

"Thanks, but no. My life may as well have ended eighteen months ago. I've been a stubborn stitch marking a wound ever since. Get on out, Kristi." He reached across her and opened the door. "I thank you."

"I wish I had given you something to be thankful for." She hopped down, hooves clicking on the concrete. She turned and looked up at him.

"More than something. Almost everything," he said and winked. The hope in Kristi's eyes sparkled in the fluorescent light. "You take care of yourself," he mumbled as he pulled the door closed and slid back behind the wheel. The engine groaned and the beast lurched as he turned towards the exit of the lot.

Kristi stood in the darkness, watching his tail lights fade like a bad tattoo. One by one the crickets ceased until the only sound in the night was the whispery hitch of her weeping.

NINETEEN

Deke kept his foot down and his eyes on the road, even though he wasn't really seeing anything. The yellow lines just blurred into a snake that danced and throbbed before him. He was certain knew who killed Lucille. He was fairly certain he was certain. He'd been thinking on it for some time now and it was the only answer. He brimmed with anger. He tasted bile as it bubbled up from his gut with a fury. He pushed the cassette into the player and the cab filled with the rich harmonies of the Statler Brothers. They pleaded with Ruby to not take her love to town. Deke sneered and spit something red and wet out the window. He kept driving while the night above just was.

IV: The Slam

"*The highway, she's hotter than nine kinds of hell...*"
—Billy Joe Shaver

TWENTY

The rig sat in the back corner of the lot. Deke sat in the cab, watching the hub. There was a light on upstairs and the dock light was on. Otherwise all was pitch. He slowly opened the door and exited the cab. Before closing the door, he reached under the seat and grabbed the wrench. He marched towards the lights. The steps were cracked and the corners clotted with wind blown fast food wrappers and nests of cigarette butts. Deke had never noticed all the trash before and he only noticed it now because he did not look up—could not look up—from the ground. He strode forward and kept his head down, counting his steps until he got to the door and yanked it open. The hinge groaned like an old man giving up his final breath. He stepped into the hub and stood by Smitty's desk as the door yawned closed. He waited . For any signs of life. The quiet grew wings and tentacles and wrapped all around him. He hefted the wrench and looked up the stairs to Boyer's office. There was still light in there and he could see a shadow by the window. He cleared his throat and started up.

At the landing, he gripped the knob and pushed it. The door swung open slowly. He could have kicked it violently or even smashed the glass with the big wrench, but he didn't. This wasn't something Deke wanted to do, it was something he had to. He stepped into the room. Boyer looked up from his desk. He swigged the last of his drink and sat the glass on the papers before him.

"Deke?" he asked, eyes wet and glassy, face red and glazed with sweat.

"I figured it out." Deke didn't so much speak the words as opened his mouth and let them flow out like lava, burning black and slow.

"Figured what?" Boyer reached for the glass and remembered it was empty so he laid his hands on the desk. He almost frowned, but it had an edge of knowing to it.

"You sent me out of town, gave me money to stay outta town all night." Deke's lips thinned until they looked like a black marker slash.

"What are you talking about?" was all Boyer managed to ask before Deke brought the wrench down on the tray of bills that squatted on the corner of Boyer's desk. Plastic and papers fluttered to the floor. Boyer pushed back from the desk, hands up in front of his chest.

"You wanted to make sure I was nowhere around. You wanted to get at her in that bad a way." Deke was reciting a script that he'd only recently written. The lines were delivered with raw emotion but no deep connect. Deke held up the wrench and leaned in. "Boyer. It was you. You took Lucille from me. It had to be you." The end was almost a question. A plea.

"Deke, you're off your nut. I would never have touched that woman. I'd never do that to someone I consider a friend. Shit, you know how few fucking friends I've got!"

Boyer started to rise, then sank back in his chair. He felt like he was under a gigantic thumb, pinned. His heart raced and he felt sweat gushing from his pores.

"They told me. They all told me. The fat thing said it was me, because of me. I thought a lot about that. That because."

Boyer coughed and spit something red on the floor. "Because is the sorriest word there is. Because anything after it is a reason. Whether it really is or not."

Deke spoke with an edge that was serrated. "You are the because. You are the reason I wasn't there." His words were threatening to become sobs, their forms dissolving.

Boyer drew in a deep breath, so deep he felt lung tissue almost tear. His eyes began to water. Every heartbeat was a firecracker going off in his chest.

"Well, Deke, I have no idea what to say. I can tell you I didn't and mean it, because I didn't, but I know you won't hear it. Won't hear a word. The siren of your grief is too loud."

Deke slammed the wrench into the filing cabinet. Boyer jumped, stopped talking, and closed his eyes for a moment, one of his last. His arm was burning.

He knew there was no way out of this alive.

He was reminded of the Bible, of all its stories involving sacrifice, Hell, that seemed to be all there was to that old book. Parables of martyrs and saints and sin and salvation.

Boyer thought of his life, all of the things he had done, wrongs he had committed. He was not a good man, but he had done good things. He was no villain but he had been the performer of unscrupulous deeds as well.

He was a gruff man, some said a coarse man, but he was a man of heart and he loved those who were owed it with ferocity. He held a key in his hand, a key to something, some place his friend needed to be. He alone was the coat to be laid across the puddle. He was the passage. He was the blade-ready lamb.

All this man needed was closure. A way out.

Maybe this was the path.

Boyer couldn't get up from the desk – his heartbeat was so fast he could feel it in his throat, and his chest and his shoulder and arm were on fire – but he felt a smile snake across his face as he raised his eyes to Deke.

"Okay," he said. "I knew you'd figure it out eventually. I'm just sorry it took so long,"

Deke looked at him and nodded, mouth tangled into some sad shape.

"I'm truly and deeply sorry," Boyer said.

The scream that filled the office was silenced by the sound of the wrench on his skull.

TWENTY-ONE

Nunnally's farm was long abandoned and the wild cornstalks were at least three feet taller than Boyer's El Dorado. Deke stood and held his hand on the open trunk. He looked down into the space, at Boyer laying there. The blood on his face was black in the moonlight.

"Remember the ashes under your tongue?" he heard himself ask. Boyer couldn't answer with the tape over his mouth but a nod worked just as well. Deke frowned as he felt a sense of déjà vu tickle him behind the ears.

"The fires, the seas and the sky..." He held up the can and pulled the cloth from the nozzle. He poured the liquid onto the man in the trunk and the man suddenly wasn't so docile.

Deke hit him with the wrench again and Boyer stilled.

"I always liked you. I never would have thought we'd come to this." Deke was crying when he struck the match. Dropped it. And when the blast of heat that blew from the trunk and singed his eyebrows, evaporated the tears from his skin. He almost thought he heard Boyer scream through the tape.

"You're forgiven."

Deke stumbled back and watched the thick smoke bellow from the trunk, his one time friend in its belly. The black smoke churned and roiled into the sky where it was swallowed by the night and no one was the wiser for it. Deke felt as hollow as a promise. He walked around to the driver's side and got into the car. He started the engine and pushed the tape into the deck. Elvis began to croon about the warm Kentucky rain as Deke slowly drove the car deeper into the rows. The smoke and flames rising higher in the night, the roar of oxygen being devoured and brittle stalks crushed under tire or igniting in the passing. The car stopped in the center of the field. A few minutes later, the explosion was a sunrise at two in the morning. Somewhere from a neighboring farm came a crow from a confused rooster.

V: The Last Run

"*There's a lot of wrong directions, on that lonely way back home*"

—Kris Kristofferson.

TWENTY-TWO

The crickets chirped and the bats chased mosquitoes under the lights of the dock. Tiny pushed the trailer doors closed and clicked the latch. He fed the lock through and sealed her up. He looked so much older. He glanced up at the moon and it looked back at him like he was nothing. Tiny made his way around to the driver's side of the truck. He stopped halfway down the trailer and put his forehead against the cold metal slats. The murmuring inside grew louder and he smacked the side once and it died down. "Tiny," a speck of a voice came from inside.

He slid his hand in between the slats and stood there until he felt someone take hold of his hand from inside. He leaned in close and whispered between the metal strips.

"You asked me that day if I ever had any cargo I knew." He squeezed the hand that had found his. Tiny wiped his eyes with his free hand and cleared his throat. "I wasn't honest with you." The large man paused and swallowed hard, "I shoulda said no, not before now."

Inside the trailer, Deke squeezed his friend's hand. He was all out of tears and was now quietly crying blood. He leaned close to the wall and whispered to his friend. A ghostly *"Thank you."*

Tiny pulled his hand away and got in the truck.

As the clock on the dash hit midnight, the truckful of the damned rolled slow down the highway, eating up the miles as though they were Halloween candy.

THE DRAWER

He stood leaning on his shovel, whistling in the graveyard. The tune was mournful and fitting of the locale. Doyle Larch was a lonely man, grown from a lonely seed. He defiantly raised himself under the saggy-lidded eye of his drunken mother. A sour woman never opened her mouth unless it was to pour in more booze or spit out more vitriol.

    Doyle was not smart by any means but he was sensitive. He knew hurt when he felt it. By the time she had finally died, his skin was thick and her barbed words would hurt him no more than a kitten's tongue. He'd smile and think of all those unfortunates who had no mama at all. He sometimes thought they were actually lucky. He floated through his existence on the periphery. A friendly phantom. Everyone in the small town knew and liked him.

    Doyle had been hired on as the cemetery caretaker, and with that title came the perk of living free in the house and needing to pay only for his groceries and any other needs. Rent and all utilities were picked up by the church. Doyle liked this arrangement as he had no head for numbers. Numbers meant bill-paying and rent-paying and budgeting his wages earned from the handyman work and odd jobs he conducted about town. This set up was easy for him. Hardly any brain work at all. He worked and spent his money, and so long as he tended the graves, kept the grass cut, the snow shoveled and the limbs gathered up after windy weather, he had a roof over his head. Easy as pie.

The house itself was a modest affair, not very large but old and sturdy, made of stones and mortar. It stayed cool in the summer months and warm enough in the winter. He mostly slept on the couch and used the downstairs bathroom. The furniture had been there when he moved in and was old and musty-smelling but comfortable, so he minded it little. There was a second floor that served mainly as storage space for the Church. It was dark and dusty and he was afraid to go up there. There were cobwebs and batwing whispers up there. Probably ghosts.

On a hazy August morning, the sun peeked around the section of the Allegheny mountains that bordered the village. Along the hill that flanked the west side of the Craghaven Methodist Church cemetery, Doyle scraped off the thick clay from the bottom of his boots on the edge of his shovel. He patted the fresh mound of dirt as flat as he could and looked at the spot where the stone would rest tomorrow. "You sleep easy, Mr. Hutch," he whispered as a scant tear crept down his cheek, like a transparent ladybug. "You was a good man and I'll miss ya. Bless you for being good to me." He walked back towards the shed, yanking the thin hanky from his back pocket and blowing his nose on the way.

The screen door slammed as Doyle came in from the storage shed with a connective cable from the mower that needed splicing. The utility knife was in the kitchen junk drawer along with the electrical tape, and he needed both. With a booted foot, Doyle pushed the door out of his way and shuffled to the far end of the counter. Pulling out the top drawer—one of those deep ones, double the depth of a regular drawer—he put the thick wire on the worn Formica and looked down. "Guess that's why they call 'em junk drawers," he mused. He began pawing through the contents: rubber bands, a few dried-up tubes of Super Glue, a half dozen batteries, a cork, paper clips, a rusty screwdriver, a pencil with a no point, toothpicks, a marble, a coupon for dish soap that was three years expired, a Ziploc baggie of washers and bolts, a few pennies, a tape measure and a roll of electrical tape- that he grabbed and laid on the counter. Elbow deep in the drawer, he took a huge handful of the mess and scattered it on the countertop. He untangled a pair of scissors from some errant binder twine, "There you are," he said when he found the knife.

Doyle smiled, picking up the utility knife and pushing the button forward. The blade poked out from the end. A razor tongue. He picked up the cable. Holding it with his left hand, he cut back and away, slowly trimming off the black rubber coating and exposing the copper wire inside. Concentration furrowed his brow as he worked. Then the blade slipped, cutting too quickly through the rubber. It slid across the knuckles of his left hand and clipped off a chunk of the ball of his extended thumb. It happened so fast he felt nothing—until he saw the blood, then the stinging throb kicked in. He reached over and grabbed a towel from the edge of the sink and squeezed it around his thumb, not before noticing about a quarter inch of flesh was missing. He looked around to see where it may have landed. He looked down and the remaining color drained from his face.

The bottom of the drawer was lined with yellowed newspaper. Old funny pages. And there was his smidgeon of thumb. It was alive, sort of, crawling around like a fat little slug. It left a thick red trail behind it that all but obliterated Dagwood and Blondie's escapades. Doyle just stared at it for a few seconds, then picked it up and laid it on the counter. It stopped squirming, becoming once more just a bloody chunk of flesh. He frowned and pushed it back into the drawer. Within a second it was slithering around again. "I'll be damned." He blushed a little at his foul tongue. He picked up the bit and unwrapped his sore thumb. He held the piece to where it had once been and watched it adhere to the digit almost as though it had never been lost. "I'll be darned. Darned to heck."

He stepped over to the fridge and opened it then leaned in and grabbed one of the fish he'd caught earlier that morning—a nice-sized bass he hadn't cleaned yet. He placed it in the drawer and waited.

Nothing.

He pushed the drawer closed and slowly pulled it open again. The fish was gasping, its tail smacking against the bottom of the drawer and its gills flaring. He filled the sink with water and put the fish in, where it promptly began to swim lazy laps.

Doyle shook his head in amazement. "It's the drawer." He scratched his chin. "It's a goshdern miracle drawer."

Over the next two days, Doyle experimented with the drawer. He squashed and resurrected a dozen roaches and beetles. He took a rat from the trap in the cellar and brought it back for a few minutes, before bashing it with a skillet and throwing it in the ditch by the road. He shot a squirrel with his pellet rifle, then resurrected it and set it free. He returned to life a road kill rabbit he had found, only to realize too late what an ill-advised move that had been. He thought the noises that poor critter made might haunt him forever. He even cleaved off his left hand pinky and put it back. Body parts only moved in the drawer, on account they can't live on their own, he surmised. He fancied he could be a great and powerful force to contend with, a god even, were he able to bring back anything larger than a cat or a groundhog. If he'd had any friends, he may have told them but he didn't so the secret stayed with Doyle.

On an early September morning, Doyle sat at the table, eating his bowl of oatmeal when the phone rang. He had a grave to dig, but it would not take long as it was a small one. The Trexler family had lost their newborn girl. It was heartbreaking to be digging a grave for a baby, but Doyle sang a little as he did it. His rusty voice filled the air. "What have I ever done… To deserve even one… Of these blessings I've known." He finished and put the tools away, then went inside to clean up.

After his shower, he walked into town for some food and supplies. He returned an hour or so later and sat the bags on the small table by the front door. He pulled out the junk drawer, removed all the bits and pieces it contained and wiped it clean with a damp dish rag. He went into the living room and came back with one of the shopping bags from town. He removed a few soft pieces of pale pink fabric and some cotton batting and lined the drawer.

He looked out the window at the small pile of dirt by the yawning hole, and smiled as the tears ran down his stubbled face. He closed the drawer and dropped the empty bag to the floor. In his calloused hands, Doyle held a new pink baby blanket.

ACKNOWLEDGEMENTS

All of the heartfelt gratitude and love I can call up goes to the one and only, John Skipp.

I've been a fan of his work since I was a teen (No, I'm not calling him old-Shut up!) and have followed and read everything he's put out there. I've since met him and befriended him and thus it just felt right when he asked about taking this novella for his Fungasm imprint, giving a second chance to a story that is very personal to me. Working with him on this I got to see a special side to the man- the editorial side wherein every single thing is under the microscope and you get an email with a single question that until he posed it you had never thought of....that kind of thing. I love you, Skipp. Goddammit, I mean it! I can never thank you enough to being my friend, a mentor, a brother and and influence on this dude that likes to write sad and strange stories.

Runner up Special thanks to all those who read this is pieces and before I subbed it anywhere. To those whose work inspires/inspired me and to those who just tolerate me and my nonsense. I thank you all. But I will now go forth and list a bunch of folks (and no doubt forget more than a few...don't be hurt, I still love you!)

Thanks to: My wife, Linda and our sons, Jim Boyer (Rest well, my Brother) Ross Boden, Mom AKA Karen Boden, Waylon Glunt, Lori Lane, Jack & Wanda Lane, Taniele Fastnacht, All of my family and In-Law family members, Chris Enterline, Elise Esposito, Alycia Hardy, Robin Noonan, Jason Butler, Aaron Dries, Catherine Grant, Jordan Krall, Joe Zanetti, Ken & Sarah Wood, Nick Contor, Michael Rogers, Bracken MacLeod, Michael Wehunt, Catherine Grant, Barry Dejasu, James Newman, Stephen Graham Jones, Richard Thomas, Mark Gunnells, Craig Metcalf, Kit Power, Sam W. Anderson, Amber Fallon, Brian Keene, Jim Vajda, Joe Fazzolari, Mike Lombardo, Chad Lutzke, Jack Ketchum (Rest thee Peacefully), Lee Thomas, Kevin Lucia, Bob Ford, Kelli Owen, Mary Sangiovanni, Ronald Malfi, Joe Ripple and Scares That Care!, Amber Fallon, Patrick Lacey, Tony Tremblay, Philip Fracassi, Kristi DeMeester, Mercedes Yardley, Ryan Johnson, Christopher Slatsky, Matthew Bartlett, Eric Beebe, Brady Allen, Jacob Haddon and his wife- Leah, Christopher Ropes, Matthew Darst, Jim McLeod and the whole GingerNuts crew, Jack Bantry, Rose Blackthorn, Gary McMahon, Chet Williamson, Scott Nicolay, Anya Martin, Chris Seibert Kevin Foster, Glenn Rolfe, Kevin Thomas, Kyle Lybeck, Jessica McHugh, Jeffrey Ford, , William Grabowski, Nathan Carson, Max Booth III, Ed Kurtz, Craig Spector, Sam Cowan, Justin Steele, Tom Monteleone, Joe Lansdale, Stephen King, Jonathan Janz, Steve Wynne, Skip Novak and probably a few dozen others that I'm forgetting at the moment.

SOUNDTRACK ACKNOWLEDGEMENTS

The following artists provided a soundtrack to the writing of this or some other type of influence on it: C.W. McCall, Loretta Lynn, Billy Joe Shaver, Waylon Jennings, Tompall Glaser, Boxcar Willie, Red Sovine, Patsy Cline, David Allan Coe, Dave Dudley, Jimmy Martin, Dolly Parton, Little Jimmy Dickens, John Prine, Grandpa Jones, Willie Nelson, Merle Haggard, Junkyard, Little Caesar, David Frizzell, Don Williams, Red Simpson, The Band, The Blasters, Hank Williams Sr, Jr and The Third, Warner Mack, Junior Kimbrough, Ronnie Milsap, Jerry Reed, Stringbean, Vince Gill, Dolly Parton, Bill Monroe, Ralph Stanley, Shooter Jennings, Johnny Cash, Blaze Foley, The Carter Family, Wilson Gil & The Wilful Sinners, Drive-By Truckers, I Can Lick Any Sonofabitch In The House, Sturgill Simpson, Shovels & Rope, Ernest Tubb, Jerry Jeff Walker, Del Reeves and The Louvin Brothers...probably a few others.

"Music is the strongest form of magic."—Marilyn Manson

ABOUT THE AUTHOR

John Boden lives a few miles from Three Mile Island with his wonderful wife and sons. They only glow in the dark sometimes. A baker by day, he spends his off time writing or watching old television shows or terrible movies. He likes Diet Pepsi, greasy food and sports ferocious sideburns. Rumor has it he's a pretty nice guy.

His work has appeared in *Borderlands 6, Shock Totem, Splatterpunk, Lamplight, Blight Digest*, the John Skipp edited *Psychos* and a few other places. His not-really-for-children children's book, *Dominoes* has been called a pretty cool thing. His other books, *Jedi Summer With the Magnetic Kid, Detritus In Love* (with Mercedes M. Yardley) and *Out Behind the Barn* (with Chad Lutzke) and are out and about and some folks dug 'em. He has a few things on the horizon and/or in the works.

Lightning Source UK Ltd.
Milton Keynes UK
UKHW010627110920
369747UK00002B/301